MODERN MYTHICAL
CREATURES

MODERN MYTHICAL CREATURES

MELODY BOWLES

MODERN MYTHICAL CREATURES

MELODY BOWLES

Contents

The Midspring Frosts

The Lady of the house calls him Jack Frost. He's never minded. It makes him feel more alive to be given a name, even if it's spoken with withering despair.

Perhaps that's why he lets Winter creep on without him. He loves the windows with their old oak frames. He loves the large grassy gardens, left to grow wild in the winter months. This old house in the depths of the countryside is safe from bright street lamps, warm exhaust fumes and double glazing. He can draw patterns of frost wherever he pleases and nothing melts them away.

The Lady shivers under piles of blankets and curses his name but makes no real effort to chase him out. She has no TV, no computer: only a corded telephone and a vast library. More books arrive every week, the covers bearing shadowy figures or foreboding titles. The library spills into every room, onto every flat surface. Jack does not draw ice on them. He is content with his window canvases and the whisper of grass in his fingers.

'Winter is awfully long this year,' the Lady tells her ginger cat, Marigold.

Jack watches her put a finger to the frost on the window. It melts against her warmth.

'Off with you, Jack Frost.'

Jack creeps closer, hoping she'll name him again. Marigold hisses. But the Lady never sees him, only feels his icy breath on the back of her neck.

'Rog?' she whispers. 'It's alright. I'll be there soon.'

Jack sighs, fed up. There's a picture of Rog in the Lady's room. It says so on the bottom: *Rog, 2004.* But he isn't sure why the Lady talks to Rog when he's clearly not there.

***

Jack must be careful. The sun is getting stronger and if it catches him, he'll...

He isn't sure if he'll really melt or if that's just a tale told to frighten creatures like him. He shrinks into the shade of a shrub one unexpectedly sunny morning and wonders if he ought to try and catch up with Winter again. It's against the order of things, him being here like this. There are other dwellings he could find inside Winter's shadow. He could always go back to that life, where he belonged but never had room to think.

As he is making up his mind, he hears a deep voice.

'What are *you* doing here, wraith?'

Jack stiffens. 'Excuse you? Are you talking to me?'

The newcomer isn't human but he's not like Jack either. He is tall and strong with hair like spring sunshine. The air around him smells sweet with pollen and he wears a coat of oak tree leaves. Jack is immediately fascinated.

'Who else?'

Such a shame petulance sours his handsome face. Jack gives him a long look. 'I live here.'

'Don't be absurd. You live with Winter and Winter is not here.'

'I do what I want,' says Jack, raising himself to his full height. He is still shorter. 'Who are you to tell me otherwise?'

'Some call me the Green Man.'

Jack scoffs. 'That's not a real name.'

'What do they call you?'

'Jack Frost.'

'Run along, Jack Frost. I am here to tend the garden and you are ruining the grass.'

'It was my garden first.'

'Do you really think you can survive here, without Winter?'

'I don't see why not,' says Jack. 'Don't think you can scare me off!'

'I don't need to,' says the Green Man, angling his face towards the sky. 'The sun will do that for me.'

A flare of jealousy goes through Jack. He'd never dare look at the sun. He shrinks back into the shade and paints angry frost spirals along tree trunks, all thought of finding Winter abandoned.

***

The shade shrinks every day as the sun rises higher in the sky. The garden with its twists and turns, its three lawns and a dozen flowerbeds, should be big enough for both Jack and the Green Man, but they seem to run into one another all too frequently.

'Must you leave a trail of ice wherever you step?' the Green Man demands.

Colourful petals sag under chilly frost crumbs where Jack has idly stepped through a flowerbed to search for shade.

'It's not like I do it on purpose.'

The Green Man snorts. 'So your excuse is ignorance, then. I should have known.'

'Why do you think they call me Jack Frost, genius? Frost is my thing. It goes where I go.'

'As soon as I bring the plants to life, you smother them again. How am I supposed to bring Spring to the garden with you here?'

'If my frost is such a problem, don't plant anything in the shade.'

'Some of my plants happen to like the shade.'

'Then they're going to get a frosting, aren't they?'

'Watch where you tread. I will not ask you again.'

'Or what? What are you going to do? Strangle me with daisy chains?'

'Don't tempt me!'

The argument puts Jack in such a sour mood that he gives up on the garden and lurks inside the house instead. He likes the noise of the Lady turning the pages of her many books. The yowl Marigold makes when her tongue hits the icy water in her bowl makes him laugh. She is such fun to tease.

'That silly old Jack Frost,' sighs the Lady. 'I shall have to get a man in to look at those pipes again.'

* * *

The Lady doesn't get in just one man.

The sun is high in the sky, the air still and balmy. Jack gets distracted following the progress of a strange furry insect with yellow stripes. It dances from flower to flower, never choosing one to settle on.

'If you could give it all a good tidy up please,' he hears the Lady say.

Is she talking to the Green Man? Can she see him? But when Jack emerges from the shrubbery, he sees a strange human unfurling a cord to a strange machine.

A roar starts up. Marigold flees. Jack watches as the stranger pushes the machine up and down the grass. He isn't sure if he's terrified or fascinated as he watches green ribbons stream in the machine's wake. The tall grass is cut to stubble. It isn't until a moment later he realises the shade has gone with it. He searches for a path back to the house but the sun carves its beams across every route. Jack will have to wait until night if he does not want to brave its shine.

He cowers in the shrubbery. Once the lawn is cut, the man fetches large silvery blades from his toolbox and advances on Jack's hiding place. Jack does not move. He feels frozen. The man reaches for one of the shrubs. Any moment, the sun will hit his face and—

A hand in his.

'Come,' insists the Green Man. 'You may borrow my coat to keep the sun off.'

'Yeah, right. You must really want to get rid of me.'

Jack shrinks back as the first shrub is cut. The sunlight hits the Green Man's face, perfectly illustrating his exasperation.

'Very well. Have it your way and perish.'

The Green Man turns away. Another shrub falls. Jack's heart hammers. He reaches out for a handful of the Green Man's coat.

'Wait,' he chokes out.

***

The Green Man leads him down tangled paths Jack half recognises. Thanks to the coat over his head, Jack can only see the ground. Even through the leafy coat, he can feel the burn of the sun.

They stop. Jack wonders if he's about to be tossed into the light so the Green Man can have the garden to himself once and for all. He pulls the coat off Jack and—they are under the branches of a tree, bare and spindly the last time Jack saw it. The plentiful leaves provide a canopy over their heads. Pin-pricks of light shine through. Not enough to hurt. Jack thinks he can see buds.

'This tree was dead!' he blurts and the Green Man rolls his eyes.

'Not dead. Merely resting while Winter passed by.'

Jack reaches for the trunk but the Green Man snatches his wrist. 'Don't even think about it.'

'But—'

'This tree is special to me. I've been tending it for many years. You may use it to shelter under, but you are not to touch a single leaf, nor tread upon its roots.'

Jack looks down at where the Green Man is holding his wrist. His grip is hard but not unpleasant.

'Why help me?'

'I don't enjoy your presence, but neither do I wish to watch you sizzle. I assume that's what would happen if the sun touched you?'

Jack shrugs. He's only heard things from others. "My

friend's cousin melted into soup in the space of half a second." That sort of thing.

'Are you telling me you don't know?'

'I'm not exactly in a hurry to test it,' Jack snaps.

An itch of resentment scratches at him, but even he knows it is not the Green Man's fault he cannot stand in the sun. He just wishes he hadn't needed rescuing, like some silly character from a tale.

'Aren't you upset about the plants being savaged?'

'They aren't being savaged. The roots are intact and the stems will grow back stronger than ever. Pruning is often necessary for healthy growth.'

The Green Man spends the next few minutes explaining, at length, the benefits of pruning. Jack thinks he should be bored but instead he is fascinated. He asks for the names of flowers, and insects too, all the things he's never seen. Things that do not grow when Winter holds the land.

Daisies and buttercups and dandelions flutter to life wherever the Green Man walks. Jack flits between jealousy and admiration like the bees between flowers. Spring holds a kinder power than Winter, he thinks. Perhaps the Green Man doesn't have a name because the humans have no reason to curse him. He does not break their houses or their machines, or their legs if they are not careful. He makes everything beautiful. If only Jack could do that.

'I did not expect a creature like you to hold an interest in such things,' the Green Man says after taking a brief pause for breath.

Then the human wielding the machine emerges from the pathway, comes close to the tree, and Jack freezes. But then he hears the tap of a cane and the Lady is there, nudging him away.

'My tree's about to blossom. It always comes so lovely, the real jewel of my garden. A wedding present from my late husband.'

Jack breathes out. He looks at the Green Man, who's standing on his toes to brush his fingers against the blossom buds. Their colour deepens from green to pink. They share a smile. Jack isn't sure what it means, but he likes it.

***

The phone won't stop ringing. It is giving Jack a headache. He is trying to draw the cherry tree in icy swirls on his favourite bay window, but he can't concentrate. Perhaps the Lady is asleep. Strange. It is Marigold's feeding time. The Lady never misses it, but he has not heard the shake of the food box.

The Lady is slumped over in her library's reading nook, book still on her lap. She is too still. Jack knows something is wrong. He bends over and touches the Lady's hand as Marigold yowls.

Ice creeps up the Lady's fingers. This time, it does not melt. She will never say his name again.

***

Not long after other humans take the Lady away, a car roars up to the house, red as poppies and louder than a lawnmower. A young woman gets out, sunglasses slung over her forehead, shirt over skinny jeans. She squints up at the Lady's house. Jack prods the car, the paint smooth and shiny under his hand. What a lovely canvas it makes.

The woman goes inside, banging the door behind her. The

Green Man appears from behind one of the rose bushes as Jack draws his first swirl on the car's windscreen.

'I wonder what she wants.'

Jack continues to shape his ice, coaxing it into whirls and veins and fronds. He doesn't care what she wants. Even though they never spoke, he misses the Lady dreadfully and he is annoyed when each human who comes is somehow not her.

The Green Man comes closer. 'You're drawing my cherry tree.'

Jack Frost shoots him a sideways glance. '*Your* cherry tree?'

'It wouldn't bloom without me.'

'So arrogant.'

'Not arrogance. Truth. I first saw it as a sapling, many years ago. I have been coming to this house for a long time.'

Jack looks around at the daisies springing from the grass, the blooms on the rose bushes. Jack's attempts at etching leaves and petals are feeble in comparison to the real thing, fragrant and alive.

'It is a beautiful likeness,' the Green Man tells him. 'I have seen your drawings on the windows too. You are quite the artist.'

It takes Jack a moment to process the compliment and when he does he isn't sure what to do with it.

'Do you want something?' he asks, suspicious.

The Green Man tsks at him. 'Why would I have need of anything from you? I only thought that perhaps we are not so different, even if our work takes different forms.'

Jack's tree does not seem in any way comparable to the real thing, but he supposes just as he's never seen blossoms, the Green Man has never seen proper frost.

The woman comes back out of the house, talking into a

tiny black slab. 'It's worse than I thought. The windows inside are all frozen up, it's bloody freezing. No wonder Auntie Rosemary copped it.'

She takes one look at Jack's work on her car and pulls the door open, scrambling around for a T-shaped wedge of plastic.

'The only way we're going to get a good price is if we gut the house. Build an extension. Make sure there's actually a working phone line. All that.'

The Green Man pulls Jack away as the woman scrapes. The cherry tree falls into a million white flakes. Once again Jack feels a thrum of irritation at not being able to draw anything that lasts.

'The garden looks a bit wild, yeah. The tree? Where?'

The ice scraper is dumped back in the car. The woman strolls through the garden, trampling daisies and buttercups. The Green Man shadows her. Jack takes a last look at the melted ice on the paving before following.

'Yeah, it's massive,' the woman says as she surveys the cherry tree. 'The roots are probably getting into the foundations of the house.'

The Green Man stiffens. Jack watches his hand clench.

'Chop it down? Yeah, probably for the best. We'll have room for a bigger extension as well. That should up the value by a few thou.'

The Green Man lets out an angry sound, somewhere between a yell and a gasp. He puts himself between the woman and the tree, but of course she cannot see him.

**

'Humans always do this in the end. They always betray

me. It is at times like this, I wish I could—' the Green Man breaks off.

They sit below the cherry tree. They aren't sure how long it's got left. Humans tend to move pretty quickly once they decide something.

'What do you wish?'

'I wish I could make humans shiver and shake the way you can. To make them feel Nature's cruelty. No, more than that. For them to remember it. For them to fear it.'

'You could enact cruelty if you wanted. You are part of Nature too.'

The Green Man shakes his head. 'All I do is make plants grow.'

'How about growing some poisonous ones?'

'There are no poisonous plants here. Not even stinging nettles.'

'Maybe we could find some.'

'They would be of little use against secateurs, even if we could. Humans are not afraid of plants. Or frost. Are humans afraid of anything?'

Jack is thrilled they have become a "we". He tries not to let it show too much and turns his mind to the question at hand.

'The Lady used to jump sometimes, when she was looking at her books and Marigold knocked something over. Are humans scared of books? But no, that can't be it...she always had so many.'

'Maybe not the books, but what's written in them. Let's have a look.'

The house feels wrong without the Lady in it. The Green

Man jumps at every click of the old pipes, every creak of the floorboards.

'There's no one here.'

'I know. I hate it. It's completely lifeless—'

As if on cue, Marigold scampers at Jack, yowling, tone much more plaintitive than usual. The Green Man shrieks. Jack hides a smile, but it disappears quickly. The cat looks sick and sad. Did the humans forget about her? Jack detours to the cupboard where he knows the Lady kept the cat food. As he's about to reach for the box, he stops. Whatever he touches freezes solid. It will be no good to Marigold like that.

'Can you help me feed the cat?'

The Green Man picks up the box and Jack shows him where Marigold's bowl is so he can shake out the weird pebbly things she eats. The cat hurriedly crunches through them and meows for more. The Green Man upends the whole box to make a miniature mountain inside her dish.

Mission accomplished, they head to the room with the books. Every shelf is full, with more piled on top. Towers of books stand high in corners. The reading nook has books piled in and around it, as if the Lady would be back to read them after all.

'Do you remember which one she was reading when she got scared?'

Jack peers at the covers and then pulls out an elegant black book with human skull patterns on the cover. He remembers thinking it beautiful in a macabre sort of way.

The Ghost Stories of MR James.

'Ghosts?' The Green Man looks puzzled.

It turns out ghosts are the spirits of the dead come back

to haunt the living. They often reside in mirrors, clocks and other household objects. Jack thinks of the Lady talking to Rog whenever she felt a cold spot.

'Humans are scared of ghosts,' the Green Man concludes. 'Where do you think we could find one? And would it help us?'

A germ of a very good idea forms in Jack's mind. He snaps his fingers. 'We don't need to. We'll pretend to be ghosts and stage a haunting. Then they'll leave the house and the tree alone.'

The Green Man sighs. 'As if it will be that easy! How are we supposed to pretend to be anything when the humans can't even see us?'

'They can see frost. They can see plants. They wouldn't usually be frightened of those things, but maybe if we change what they see...this could work!'

'They'll probably call some sort of ghost hunter and we'll be back to square one.'

'Yeah, well...we're not *actually* ghosts. A ghost hunter isn't going to touch us.'

The Green Man remains sceptical, but in the end Jack gets him to admit he doesn't have any better ideas. They spend the rest of the night reading ghost stories, noting their favourite ideas for hauntings and laying out a plan for just what would happen to the next human who stepped into the Lady's house.

Marigold comes in, looking much more content than she did earlier. She climbs onto the Green Man's lap and purrs. Jack feels mildly put out as *he* was the one who remembered she needed feeding. All the same, her dozy presence calms the room. The Green Man soon joins her in sleep, half holding on to his book. Jack, being the more nocturnal sort, stays up to read some more.

He's glad he didn't follow Winter.

***

The Green Man goes to work the next day, fashioning walls of thorns from the usually tidy rose beds. The bright sun bolsters his powers and Jack loves to watch him coax the plants to life under his fingers. The thorns wrap around every doorway, barricading the house.

As for Jack, he draws frost on the inside of every window, to avoid hurting the roses. He freezes up every tap, every radiator, every pipe he can find. Spiders scuttle in his wake and he stops to watch them, amused.

Marigold lounges around showing only languid curiosity, probably because the Green Man has dumped another packet of food into her bowl. When a mouse scurries across the floor, she merely blinks at it.

They meet at the cherry tree once their preparations are complete. It's in full, pink blossom. The Green Man's hair is littered with fallen petals. Jack has never seen anything so beautiful. He desperately hopes their plan will work.

'I suppose now we must wait,' says the Green Man and from the blackest part of the shade, Jack nods.

***

They don't have to wait long. The red car drives in the very next morning with a large van in tow. Jack watches as the same woman from before gets out of the car and two lads, tall and strong, get out of the van.

'Wow, Mum!' says one of them, eyeing the house. 'You never said it looked like *this*. It's beautiful!'

The woman blinks at the thorny bushes, so thick one can barely tell there's a house beneath them.

'This must be some kind of joke, it can't have grown like this in *two days*.'

The boys shrug. The front steps are impassable. They try to bat the branches aside and end up with torn sleeves and pricked arms.

Jack steals into the lady's car through the open window, spreads his cold hands over the steering wheel and the pedals. The longer he stays, the colder it gets. He watches the humans unload a large box of tools, searching for something to cut a path.

Jack waits in the car a couple of minutes more, making sure everything is coated in a thick layer of ice.

When he gets inside the house, the humans are chasing Marigold, trying to get her inside a small wiry cage. She darts up the stairs and they follow, heading exactly where Jack wants them to go.

The Lady's bedroom. Her bed is unmade, her shiny pots and tubes and hairbrush laid out neatly on her dresser, alongside a vase of wilting flowers. Everywhere smells like her perfume. There is a picture on her bedside table of a smiling gentleman beneath the cherry tree. *Rog, 2004.* Her presence in this room is unmistakable.

A large, ornate mirror hangs on one wall. The edges are curled with intricate silver waves. Jack never touched the mirror while the Lady was alive, out of respect for its silvery shine.

Now—Jack has left a single word on the mirror, painstakingly etched into ice.

LEAVE

'Kids,' says the mother. 'A cruel joke by kids who must have got in and done this—'

'The village is miles away,' says one of the brothers. 'And Aunt Rosemary was kind of a loner. Not a lot of people knew she was here...'

Jack lets out a deliberate puff of icy breath against the woman's cheek and watches as she tries not to shiver. Then he deliberately puts his hand on the back of her neck, making sure she can feel every finger.

She screams. The boys jump.

'There's someone here,' she says, voice quavering. 'Auntie? Is that you, Auntie?'

'Don't be daft, Mum! Let's get some light in here!'

The other boy goes to the window and before Jack can think about what's happening, the curtains are thrown open. Sunlight floods the room. There are not enough roses outside to break up the light, which hits Jack with full force.

To say it burns is a gross understatement. Every part of him feels like it's being fed to a raging fire. Jack cannot see, cannot move, cannot think. There's some murmuring from the humans, and yowling. He isn't sure if it's him or Marigold until he hears a metallic clunk, a cage slamming shut. The light is dazzling. He can't stop looking. His awareness fizzles until—

Shade.

'Oh no you don't, Jack,' he hears the Green Man say. 'I will not let such a foolish misstep take you from m—from here.'

Jack blinks back into himself. The roses have grown back over the window, so thick and fast they burst into the room in a tangle of leaves and spikes. The Green Man is next to him, the leaf coat around his shoulders.

The humans stare. Jack puffs out enough breath to cause a gust of freezing air. He draws their attention to the mirror again and deliberately writes into the ice, right where they can see the path of his fingertips.

LEAVE

'I'm putting this on Youtube,' declares one of the boys.

'We're only here to collect your things,' says the woman. 'We can't just leave them here.'

TAKE + LEAVE, writes Jack.

The woman's eyes bulge. She wrenches the mirror off the wall. Checks the back, checks the inside of the frame. Bangs her fist on it.

'You're dead,' she sobs. 'I...I don't understand.'

'Leave,' Jack hisses in her ear and though she can't hear him, she can feel the shape of the word from his cold, cold breath.

The flowers lurch into life next, leafy tendrils snatching a boy's wrist. He yells and shakes it off. The vase smashes onto the carpet.

'I'm so not down with being attacked by flowers! Freaking hell!'

'Ghosts aren't real,' says the other brother and then gasps when the Green Man slowly presses a thorn into his palm.

In the end, the only thing the humans take with them is Marigold. They even leave the red car after it won't start. The house is left in blessed silence.

Jack's skin is red but he seems otherwise unharmed. The Green Man fusses, pressing aloe vera leaves from the Lady's pots to the burns. It's unnecessary, but it's nice. So he doesn't protest.

'I know I wanted them to be frightened but...do you think we went too far?' the Green Man asks.

Jack shakes his head. 'Think about the tree. What would have happened if we hadn't acted?'

'Yes. The Lady Rosemary loved the tree. She would have wanted it to stay, I think.'

***

More humans come, but they refuse to stop for long. Jack and the Green Man repeat the core of their plan—words on icy surfaces, plants that snatch and grab at stray limbs. It's misusing their powers, probably, but Spring is too busy with other matters and Winter is absent.

Eventually, humans stop coming. The house stands empty. But not unloved. The Green Man grows plants up its walls, through its floors. The plaster and brick give way to earth and leaf and flower. He teaches Jack to use his frosty touch on poisonous plants and pests to help foster new growth. Jack has never used his powers for such a purpose before. He likes it. Maybe even loves it.

Together, they turn the house and garden into a green paradise. Something new from something old.

'I'll need to go soon,' the Green Man says when the days grow shorter and the nights chilly.

Jack's heart sinks. 'Why?'

'I'm not meant to be here when Winter comes.'

'I'm not meant to be here. It's turned out alright for me.'

The Green Man smiles, so gentle and fond Jack doesn't know what to do with himself.

'Don't leave. Please.'

The Green Man raises his eyebrows. 'You sound sincere, but as it is you speaking I must check. Is there a punchline? A careless quip yet to come?'

'I mean it,' says Jack. 'With me here, there's no need to worry about the frost.' And when the Green Man still looks sceptical, he leans up and in. The Green Man is so warm Jack's ice melts on his lips. He doesn't shiver. They look at each other for a long moment.

Jack hopes. He's been doing that a lot lately. He likes it.

When humans come back to the house, it's not to remake it. They come because it's the only place where roses bloom, even when the land is in the grip of Winter.

The Star

In the grasslands of Sussex lay a pool called a knucker-hole. Anything dropped down there—coins, twigs, glasses, dogs—would never again see the light of day.

'Y'know Lydia Randolph? I made her a star!' said Jimbo Pulk to the barman.

Jimbo jabbed a trembling finger at a framed poster of a blonde Amazon toting a gun. The pub owners were movie buffs and the theme ran throughout the building. Toilets with stars on the doors. Film reels dancing across the ceiling.

'That's nice, mate.'

'And him, Enrique Douglas. He was in my film first!' A poster with a cowboy. Bushy beard. 'They don't write, they don't call. Too busy for me now. Even though no one had time for them before me.'

'Uh-huh.'

'I can make anyone a star with my films. I can make you a star! You wanna be a star?'

'I'll call you a cab.'

'Stick your cab! I'm fine!'

'OK, sir. We're closing now, so if you could just—'

Jimbo staggered out into the rain. On the way back to his

luxury barn conversion, he got a little confused. Discombobulated. He really should have taken a cab. He ended up tramping through unfamiliar fields, where he found a deep pool of black water.

'Be...ware,' read Jimbo. The rest of the sign was smudged. He had found the knuckerhole.

***

'Why do you want to work for Laura's Pharmaceuticals?'

Matilda smiled her best smile and pressed her hands against her neatly-ironed skirt. She couldn't say "Because my mum told me I need to get a real job and she's right", so she did what anyone would. She lied.

'I've always loved coming to your store. It's very...well-organised. And what you do is very important. People need their medicines.'

Her interviewer's face looked like a shirt that hadn't been ironed. She read the next question off her sheet.

'What experience can you bring to the team?'

This woman had read her CV, surely. 'I played a leading role in the soap opera, *Easterdale Street* for several years. I think acting is very important when you're in customer service.'

'Why?'

Matilda began to sweat. 'Because you have to pretend to like people. Or like they're not annoying you when they are. That sort of thing.'

'I see. Do you think we *pretend* to care about our customers?'

'Er, no! Of course you care! But you must have some that get on your nerves, right?'

'Hmm,' said the interviewer. 'You look different than on the telly.'

Matilda didn't get the job. When she went to the pharmacy to pick up some paracetamol the next week, she saw the new girl getting trained behind the counter. Employers didn't even bother to send out rejection letters anymore. Too busy for that nonsense. Well, she was busy too! She'd been invited to audition for the lead role in a no-budget fantasy film. Her pay made peanuts look generous, but it was a job. So there.

***

The film crew bustled around Matilda, setting up cameras and testing audio equipment. In the production, a muddy pool played the part of the "knuckerhole", a bottomless pit home to an angry creature called a "knucker".

Matilda was playing the princess that pissed it off. Her lines were so lacklustre not even perfect delivery could save them. She muttered to herself anyway, testing the emphasis on each word. Matilda secretly loved the cheesy moments in films where the characters turned to the camera and said the perfect one-liner before stomping the villain. She had been waiting for a moment in her career where she could deliver a line like that. She was yet to find one and this script was no different. Her character remained perfectly ladylike and perfectly boring, even when the knucker threatened to swallow her whole.

Penny, the runner, scuttled over. 'Hey, Mattie. You want egg and cress or tuna mayo?'

'Ugh. Again?'

'Our budget is pretty limited, I'm afraid. That's why we're all the way out here to do the special effects, to keep things cheap.'

Penny's headset squawked something at her. She made an

apologetic face before running off again. Matilda looked at the proffered packages, their contents already wilting, and took the egg and cress. It looked safer. Behind her, a round of greetings. Will had arrived at last, just in time to receive his sorry sandwich. She knew him from drama school, but they'd never had a proper job together. Will was an average actor but kept getting cast because he was easy on the eyes and nice to people. Not that she could really begrudge him that. They all played the game and Matilda had been playing it longer than most. At fifteen, she'd been cast as the long-lost daughter of a popular soap bitch in *Easterdale Street*. Her career hadn't reached such giddy heights since.

The crew were like the mice in *Cinderella*, diligently spiriting this or that from the vans. An impromptu picnic table was set up so they could eat.

'Simply delicious,' said Will through a mouthful of sandwich, like he had every other day of filming. There was a crease on his flawless forehead. He didn't chew. He gulped. It was a good job he wasn't playing the part of man-enjoying-his-sandwich.

Matilda raised an eyebrow. 'You always say how much you like the tuna. That's why I always save it for you.'

She couldn't help teasing. If you bumped into former colleagues in a bar or a coffee shop after production wrapped, it was never the same. She may as well enjoy the strange closeness that came with being driven out in the middle of nowhere to film a shouting match by a muddy bog.

'Very thoughtful.' He gave her a watery smile. 'I might just save the other one for later.'

'Good idea. Who knows how long we're going to be out here in the mud?'

'I did wonder...what kind of shoes is our princess wearing?'

Matilda lifted her skirts to knee-level so she could show off her polka-dotted wellies.

'Oh. Sexy.'

She smiled. Nothing like light flirtation with a dash of mockery to pass the time.

At least the characters' extended stupidity and the production team's obsession with "authenticity" meant Matilda could afford rent. After this, she was back to endless audition halls and "We're looking for someone fresher for the role". Like Matilda had gone off or something, and her career was the equivalent of a wilting sandwich.

'What's your next project?' she asked Will, hoping he might be able to commiserate. Instead, he lit up.

'I'm in an episode of this Netflix period drama. My agent said it could be my big break.'

'Congratulations.'

Of course. He'd look great in stupid regency sideburns. His star was rising, hers falling. On this project, they'd just happened to meet in the middle.

Matilda couldn't look at him. If she did, she might start crying.

Luckily, she was saved by the producer, Jimbo Pulk approaching their table. It had been his idea to cast her, so she flashed her best smile.

'Good lunch?' he asked.

Matilda took an enthusiastic mouthful of foul sandwich and nodded frantically.

'Good, good. Today's going to be fun. The effects will knock your socks off. But we can only do them here because of the reflections from the knuckerhole and the way the light falls through the trees and—'

Matilda tuned out. She didn't care about the technicalities. Whatever Jimbo was cooking up, it was her job to make it look real.

***

Matilda tried to look beseeching.

'Sir, I ask you to turn back. I make this sacrifice willingly, to save my people.'

'Nah,' said Will. 'Your old man says if I kill the knucker, I get to marry you. No sacrifices necessary.'

'Cut!' yelled the director. 'Nice delivery, but Mattie, you have a hair in your mouth. Again, from the top!'

She shuddered. Her stomach felt like it was floating. Strange. She never got stage fright.

'Mattie?' She should have told Will to stop calling her that three days ago. Now everyone was doing it and it was far too late to stop them.

'Ready when you are,' she said, putting on her best smile. Princesses didn't hide their long, flowing dresses under anything as common as a coat, so it was an effort not to shiver. Any rays from the afternoon sun were pale, hampered by gathering clouds.

They went through the scene a few more times. The words sounded more nonsensical with every take. Matilda remembered her drama tutor saying everyone wished they sounded like they were in a film or a play. Real conversation was painful. Too much stumbling, too much stop-starting, too much puzzling over what the other really meant. Her princess knew what the hero would say and had the perfect response at the ready. If Mattie had a boyfriend ready to fight a monster, she wouldn't be egging him on. She'd be telling him to run for his life. Especially if, like Will, he made her believe a smile really could be heart-melting.

Will didn't have anything better to work with. He was supposed to play a normal bloke, the kind you'd want to have a pint with. Unfortunately, the way he said "Alright?" was all wrong. He made it sound like an actual inquiry rather than a lazy greeting.

Matilda struggled to focus. She definitely felt odd. Queasy. But she had a job to do.

'Poison you say!' Matilda gasped, a hand to her breast. 'How cowardly! Any man who wishes to wed me should fight nobly. Where is your bl-bla-bleurgh!'

Mattie's legs fell out from under her as she threw up.

Oh god. Oh god. And it was on camera. She was so very, very fired. No one in the film industry would ever want to work with her again and the people at Job Centre Plus were going to laugh her out of the office.

'Mattie!' Will crouched beside her and held back her hair, which was far more noble than killing a knucker-dragon-whatever with a sword. At least in her book. She wondered if Will would still flirt with her now she'd chundered on his shoes.

She stumbled away over to the pond or knuckerhole or whatever it was. Being sick in the mud was better than the grass. Probably. She watched the water ripple and flex. Damn. Where the hell had Penny sourced the sandwiches from? A mad scientist's laboratory? They'd looked past their best, but they hadn't tasted that bad...

'Hang on,' said Will. He had retrieved his sandwich packet. 'I'm pretty sure this best before date is for last year.'

The water bubbled over the knuckerhole, like a saucepan. Steam rose up. A shape formed, murky before the steam cleared. Scales gleamed in the sunlight, turning its weak rays into bright shimmering lights.

There was a beat while they all stared. Someone screamed. Someone else hushed them.

Matilda had been wondering what a "knucker" was and now she knew. It had a long, serpentine body made of steam and mud. Its eyes were cat-shaped and sickly yellow. When it opened its jaw, she saw a deep void studded with shark teeth.

A rumbling sound came from the knucker. The water whirled as it roared. Matilda stumbled back. Watched as the line of its body streamed towards her, jaws open. Jimbo's special effects were very realistic. Not a green screen in sight.

'Princesses,' it rasped, 'never learn.' Its dank breath touched her cheek.

Matilda was silly to be scared. This monster was just an effect and she knew what to do. It was right there in the damned script, which she'd spent a week learning top-to-bottom. She didn't have the right props, so for this take she'd just have to improvise.

Iridescent knucker drool splashed her cheek as its jaw unhinged, revealing the dark cave of its throat. But no way was she letting this stupid special effect ruin her moment. This was *her* scene and she wasn't going anywhere.

Will, bless him, ran towards her. Just like a romantic hero.

But she only needed one thing. She seized the sandwich from his grasp.

'Oi, you knucker!' she yelled. 'Eat this!'

She hurled the discarded sandwich into the beast's gaping maw. Its jaws came down as it swallowed the tuna monstrosity. Its eyes rolled into the back of its head. It coughed and spluttered and coughed and fell back into its hole. There it sank back below the mud, tongue lolling from its mouth. 'Nooo!' it wailed, voice trailing off weakly. 'Not poison!'

Matilda wiped her cheek and sank into the grass.

All was quiet apart from the cameras whirring.

It would turn out to be one of the biggest moments in Matilda's illustrious acting career and remembered as iconic in years to come.

Will stared, mouth slightly agape. He still clutched the empty sandwich packet. Matilda laughed. 'Do you mind if I brush my teeth before I kiss you?'

'Beautiful improvisation,' hollered Jimbo from his position behind the camera. 'Absolutely smashed it. Even better than scripted! You two have done a bang-up job.'

***

Later.

Jimbo set down his backpack and brought out three freshly baked pies: beef, fish and chicken. He laid them out on the edge of the knuckerhole. The moon shone brightly on the water.

'You overplayed dying,' Jimbo said. 'It was completely corny.'

A shape rose from the mist.

'It was my moment,' said the knucker. It devoured the first pie with a contented "mmm" noise. The snap of its teeth made Jimbo take a step back.

'I know, but next time stick to the script. Which wasn't death by sandwich. You want to be *scary*, right?'

'Fine,' said the knucker. 'What's the next play?'

'Do you want to be the imaginary friend of a young boy, the close confidant of a villainess or the terrifying nightmare vision of a drug addict?'

'All of them,' declared the knucker. 'It's good I did not eat you. These plays are *much* more fun. And I will be famous!'

'That's right. I'll make you a star.'

Jimbo had said those words so many times, to so many young actors and actresses that they rolled off his tongue without a second thought. Even when he was drunk and lost and about to be devoured by a monster.

The Adventure of the Loch Ness Monster

Jane lagged behind Lizzie, wishing she'd put on tougher shoes. Every bump in the path bruised the soles of her feet. They were lightly buzzed on whiskey after handing in their final year dissertations and Jane's all-nighter was definitely coming back to bite her. She took another swig to fend it off.

Lizzie, a good few metres ahead, stopped to whirl her arms. The wind blew her hair out in a golden arc.

'You can't catch me!' she hollered down at Jane.

Jane held Lizzie's whiskey bottle teasingly over the crest of the hill. Lizzie came hurtling towards her with an anguished cry. 'Anything but the alcohol!'

They continued up the path together, Edinburgh spread out below them. Over three years of studying, it was a view Jane had seen countless times. The shapes of the rooftops were familiar, but the sky was always different. Today the clouds were perfect sheep puffs, creating dappled shadows over the city.

When they reached the top, other students milled about with their own drinks. Lizzie chose a free spot in the sunshine and flopped down on the grass. They took a moment to regain their breath, watching the climbers determined to scale the very last sharp incline to Arthur's Seat proper.

'We did it,' said Jane. They clinked bottles. 'Can't believe uni's really over.'

Jane remembered Freshers' Week, the constant cacophony of stalls and banners and leaflets. She'd never been able to choose much of anything before and suddenly she'd had to decide if she was a gamer, baker, feminist, hockey player...or all of them. Her room mates had ditched her hours before and she'd been hot, flustered and in dire need of a sit down.

Every single bench had been occupied. In the end, she'd admitted defeat and plonked herself next to a tall blonde girl staring into a pizza box like it held all the answers to the universe.

'Hi,' the blonde girl had said. 'This pizza is free.'

'...Good? Good for you.'

'It's my fourth free pizza. Ten minutes ago I thought I wanted another one.'

Despite her mood, Jane had laughed. Then Lizzie had regaled her with the Saga of the Free Freshers' Pizza, a grand quest ending in misery and stomach ache. And thus began their friendship of pizza sharing, pub going and adventuring to random places in Edinburgh depending on Lizzie's random whims. These activities had been interspersed with intense stints in the library when either of them had an essay due.

'I couldn't have done uni without you,' Jane said, savouring the wind in her hair, the whiskey on her tongue.

'That's not what you said when we got locked in the library

with a near empty vending machine and you lost the coin toss for the chocolate muffin.'

'OK, that's true—'

'Or when we got so lost we couldn't find a bus stop and neither of our phones had any data so you had to call a taxi just to get us home.'

'Alright, so more like you couldn't have done it without me.'

'Cheers for saving my life, on multiple occasions.'

They clinked again.

'I talked to Mum last night,' said Lizzie and Jane braced herself. Lizzie talking to her mum didn't ever end well. 'She's agreed to lend me money for the detective agency start-up. Sort of.'

'Sort of? What does that mean?'

'I have to prove myself first,' said Lizzie. 'She's given me a case. And, well. I wondered if you'd like a job? Gonna need the Watson to my Holmes, baby!'

'Oh, so I have to grow a moustache?'

'If it pleases you, dear Jane. But seriously, what do you think? Are you in?'

'Is it dangerous? I really don't know much about this private investigator stuff...'

'It's not dangerous. It's talking to people or observing them, figuring out if they're hiding things. Stuff someone with a degree in psychology might be good at, you know?'

'I don't have my degree *yet*.'

'It's good enough for me. And I think when you hear the case, you'll want in. It's a good'un.'

Sometimes it was hard to tell when Lizzie was being

serious or joking around. But. It wasn't like Jane had anything else to do apart from job hunting and surely after three
years of hard study (kind of, most of the time), she deserved
a break. A diversion to stop her wondering what nine-to-five
based tyranny lay on the other side of summer.

'What's the case?'

'So. Have you ever heard of the Loch Ness Monster?'

'Lizzie. I'm Scottish. I think you can assume I've heard of
the Loch Ness Monster.'

'Yes. Good. So, my mother wants me to find it. If I do, I
get the money to start the agency.'

Jane gaped. Struggled to find words. Finally, she settled
on, 'That bitch.'

'Tell me about it. She should really just give me the money,
before she blows it on facelifts. Her eyebrows haven't moved
in years, you know.'

Jane snorted as Lizzie began to describe, in detail, her
mother's other latest sins which included getting into a Twit-
ter fight with a journalist about the ethics of dogs wearing
pyjamas. She wasn't sure if it was giddiness from alcohol,
buzz from submitting her dissertation, or Lizzie's sparkling
presence that made her agree to get up at the ungodly hour
of 9:30 am the following day so they could begin the search
for Nessie.

***

They had Costa coffees, every Taylor Swift CD they
owned (all of them, most twice) and a ten-year-old sat nav
which Lizzie held one-sided arguments with. The hire car
was bright red, spacious and had plenty of va-va-voom in the
engine.

'So. The Loch Ness Monster,' said Lizzie. 'Let's compile what we know.'

Jane sipped her coffee, trying to beat off her early morning fugginess. 'Big monster. Rumoured to live in Loch Ness, goes by the alias Nessie. Most people think of a long, shadowy neck sticking out of the water. That photo was of a model made of wood and a toy submarine. So, a hoax.'

'That's what the photographer's mates said but he never confessed. What else?'

'First popular modern sighting was in 1933 by the Spicer couple as they drove on the newly opened road next to the loch. They said Nessie crossed the road in front of them. She had an enormous whale-like body, a long neck and no legs.'

'Sort of like a really big snake.'

'Or perhaps an eel? When scientists conducted a DNA study of the loch a couple of years back, they only found eel DNA. No reptiles, no sharks or anything else. Just eels.'

Jane scrutinised the pictures of "Nessie" they'd found on Instagram again. The selfies were unclear and awkwardly angled, as if the posers hadn't time to perfect them. She could see a shadow of something long and turquoise and the gleam of two beady eyes in the background. The posts were tagged with #meetnessieatlochness. Clicking the hashtag revealed a wall of similar photos.

Jane tried to find obvious clues the pics were fake, but the creature in the background seemed to move from picture to picture. Its mouth sometimes hung open in what appeared to be a cute grin, revealing long sharp teeth.

Lizzie had tried messaging a few of the photographers, but none had replied. It seemed they weren't up for telling them how they'd come to take the photos. The whole thing was probably a scam. Nessie bagged Scotland over a million quid every year so it wasn't hard to see the incentive.

'Lizzie, I think the photos are next to a giant screen or something. The world's been looking for Nessie for nearly one hundred years. They haven't found her.'

'Maybe they weren't looking in the right place.'

'I'm pretty sure they were looking in the loch—'

'Alright, alright. I get it. We can be 99% sure these photos are just some weird tourist campaign. But the 1% is still worth investigating. Just to be sure.'

***

The loch's waters were grey-blue. Gentle waves shimmered beneath green hills. The shadow of a crumbling castle stood to one side, the only man-made thing in sight. Jane took a deep breath of cold, crisp air. She felt like she'd walked into a landscape painting.

Lizzie marched off towards a shed on the bank behind them proclaiming itself a "Tourist Information Point", without even a second glance at the scenery. Jane reluctantly followed, wondering if she could convince Lizzie to drive to the castle later on.

Inside the shed was a man, middle-aged, with a bright red beard and an array of screens showing various views of the loch. A coffee machine stood in one corner. It was the shiniest thing in the room.

'Two coffees, please,' said Lizzie.

The man tore his eyes away from the screens. 'Will you watch that for me?' he said. 'Thought I saw something move a wee second ago.'

'No problem,' said Lizzie. 'Looking for something, are you? Like, say, a monster?'

'Laugh all you want. If I get a sighting on camera, I'm quids in. The media will be begging me for it.'

'We're looking for the monster too,' said Lizzie. 'Or more accurately, concrete evidence she exists.'

'You and every other tourist in town.'

He presented them with two paper cups of instant coffee. Jane scrounged up some money while Lizzie swept her gaze over the screens, images blurred from the intense zoom of the cameras.

'Don't suppose you know anything about this?' asked Lizzie, showing him one of the Instagram snaps.

The man's face darkened. 'Bloody grifters. Making a killing with their animatronics while people like me do the real work looking for Nessie and get paid diddly squat.'

'Apart from the massive profit margins on the coffee,' said Lizzie, looking him up and down. 'But you spend it all in winter when trade is dead, don't you? You spend all day watching the screens and all night playing footage back in case you've missed anything. You survive off Pot Noodles and sausage rolls, hoping one day Nessie leaps out of the water like a dolphin.'

'Lizzie!' hissed Jane. When she started deducting all tact went straight out of the window.

But the man was laughing. His face looked much kinder when it was mirthful.

'I like a girl who tells me it straight,' he said. 'Go on, tell me how you worked all of that out.'

'It's obvious,' huffed Lizzie. 'You've got an expensive

portable heater plugged in which you must use in winter. On the window sill is a row of empty noodle pots, some of which contain plants. Very creative. Your eyes are red and watery. Judging by the way you squint, you're short-sighted. You spend a lot of time doing screenwork but you're too proud to admit it's time to go to Specsavers.'

He clapped. 'Proper little detective we got here.'

'These monitors look old. She's right. You've been here for years,' said Jane. 'You really believe Nessie is real, don't you?'

'Course she is. Or…there's *something* in these waters, I'll bet my life on it. Look at this.'

He started clicking around on his boxy computer screen. He brought up a series of photographs.

'Look at this,' he said, pointing to a barely visible mark on the water. 'Bubbles.'

He magnified the image but it still remained blurred beyond comprehension. It was in grey and white, which Jane assumed meant it was taken in low lighting.

'Let's look at the next one,' he said. A near identical image, the same mark. And another. And another.

'That could be anything,' said Jane.

'Always at the same time,' he said. 'Seven thirty-three p.m., every day for the past six weeks. What do you make of that?'

Lizzie's face changed from contemplative into the grin Jane both loved and dreaded.'Guess when the photos on Insta were uploaded?'

Jane stared. 'No. Not at the same time. It can't be.'

'19:34, 19:34, 19:35, 19:32…I could go on,' said Lizzie. 'Funny, that.'

She turned back to the man in the hut. 'Where do I find these grifters? I'm in the mood to be swindled.'

***

'It's probably just a coincidence. And anyway, that mark didn't look like anything. I bet you could find it in other pictures as well, if you looked hard enough. He's obsessive, seeing things that aren't there.'

'I thought you were supposed to be helping,' Lizzie grumbled. Her grip tightened on the steering wheel.

'I'm just trying to be realistic.'

'Jane. I love you and you're my partner in crime forever. But I already get enough of the "be realistic" shit from everybody else in my life. Please can you be on my side? Just this once?'

'What do you mean "just this once"? I'm always on your side, you daft cow.'

'Moo!'

'Moo to you too.'

They followed directions to a strip of hotels-turned-tourist-attractions in a village close to the loch side. Posters stuck to lamp posts led them past the bigger attractions (all of them busy) to a vivid shop front emblazoned with the words THE NESSIE EXPERIENCE in a swirly font. A bright turquoise image of Nessie coiled round the window. Her head looked like an eel's, all bulging eyes and pointed teeth. Maybe the so-called grifters had also read the news about the DNA studies. Jane could respect that.

Lizzie held up her phone to compare with the Instagram photos. Jane tilted her head to take a look too. The creature in the photo didn't look dissimilar to the one on the front of the shop.

They exchanged glances before pushing the door open. The inside was an explosion of colour. The walls were azure and fake flowers clustered in corners—magenta, orange, yellow. One wall held a scarlet bookcase filled top-to-toe with travel books. Berlin, Portugal, Copenhagen, Toronto... Once you looked past the Instagrammable parts, Jane realised the unit could barely hold three people comfortably.

'Good afternoon, ladies! Here for the tour your Insta feed won't ever forget?' said the young man on the front desk. Skinny, blonde, round rimless glasses. A scarlet fedora, even indoors, with matching suspenders. A bit much, Jane thought.

'Is this you?' asked Lizzie, flashing the Instagram photo.

'That's us! Hashtag meet Nessie at Loch Ness!'

People who said the word "hashtag" made Jane cringe.

'Aha! Judging from your youthful qualities and the way you have been sneakily browsing Tripadvisor on your phone instead of writing emails, you must be here on work experience,' exclaimed Lizzie.

He tilted his head quizzically. 'I'm actually the business manager and head tour guide.'

'Oh. Well. Tickets for two,' said Lizzie with far less embarrassment than the situation warranted.

'And on your tour, we're going to meet Nessie. Just to be clear. The real deal from the photos,' said Jane.

'Correct. If you're a sceptic, I don't blame you. But how will you know for sure if you don't come and see?'

Jane let out a "hmph", knowing pithy sales patter when she

heard it. Then the guide named a sum that made Jane blink twice. He said it as casually as if it were the price of two coffees. Lizzie threw down her card with a flourish.

Jane fidgeted, wanting to pay her share but not quite able to offer. The balance of her bank account was much closer to zero than she'd like. Her student loan was finished and she wasn't sure she'd be able to find a job anytime soon. Psychology graduates were never in the highest demand, a hard truth her parents had tried to warn her about.

'Sorry miss, your card's been declined.'

'Try it again,' Lizzie demanded.

Oh no. This was a dance Jane knew all too well. After a chorus of beeping, the man shook his head.

'Declined.'

'That old witch,' Lizzie muttered. 'She's cut me off! Again!'

She turned to Jane with round, pleading eyes. Jane swallowed. The word "no" was on her lips. Almost. But then she said, 'I can get this.'

It didn't feel good, watching the number on the screen. Her fingers shook as she typed the PIN.

'That's all booked in for you. Come back this evening and we'll be delighted to let you meet Nessie.'

'Fabulous,' said Lizzie. She slung her arm around Jane's shoulders and steered them out of the shop. It wasn't enough to stop the dull warning note of dread buzzing in Jane's head.

***

Jane leant against the car, looking out at the loch. It should have been peaceful. Except Lizzie paced a few feet away, yelling into her phone.

'You told me to investigate! For which I need funds! Come on, Mum, it was you who put me on this mad quest.'

Jane did not want to think about money. If she looked into the loch for long enough, maybe she could think about peaceful things. Like the glide of a graceful swan or the gentle bend of reeds in the wind...

'Yeah, well, I needed those shoes!'

It would be fine. She'd get a job soon. Whatever job she could. Waitressing. Shelf stacking. Warehouse picking.

'That's not fair, that trip to Spain was *essential* for my studies!'

Lizzie would feel betrayed if she knew how much Jane sided with her mother sometimes.

Lizzie said. 'Fine. Love you,' in the tersest way possible and clicked off the call.

Jane didn't look at her as she came back. 'Are you back in business?'

Lizzie sniffled. 'Nope. She said she was serious this time and I've got a perfectly reasonable amount in my account for expenses.'

That was new. Bloody typical that when Jane needed paying, the cash stopped coming.

'Right. OK.'

'She's such a cow,' said Lizzie. Jane angled a glance at her.

'Are you crying?'

'No,' Lizzie lied. Then, 'I hate arguing with her even when she's being so tight.'

'Maybe we should cancel the tour. It's not going to be anything real. It's going to be a robot or a moving screen or a puppet.'

'But we came all this way and I will pay you back. You trust me, don't you?'

Jane thought of everything they'd been through in the last three years. The time Lizzie wanted to try absinthe and Jane had been the one to drag her home. Lizzie's first time in London, where she'd insisted on hiring Boris bikes. They'd almost caused a black cab pile up until Jane actually read the road signs and got them back on track. The time Lizzie insisted peanut butter on noodles would be delicious. She'd been so crestfallen at the resulting mess that Jane bought her a takeaway.

Lizzie got them into trouble. Jane got them out. That was the way it was. The way it always would be. But somehow, despite it all, Jane always had the best fun with her.

Jane patted her shoulder. 'Alright. Let's do it. We'll get a story and some cool pics to share. It can be a way to celebrate our graduation.'

Lizzie jolted. 'Did you see that?'

Jane turned back to the loch. The water rippled, as if something large had broken the surface but there were no birds or boats. They stared into the loch for a long time, hoping for a glimpse of something magical.

***

They arrived at the shop a couple of minutes late because Jane had taken them on a walk that was longer and more winding than intended. The chap from earlier greeted them with enthusiasm that almost didn't seem canned. His hat and suspenders were now accented with turquoise Nessie squiggles.

'Ah, perfect! That's everybody! My name is Mitch, I'll be

your guide. Thank you so much for joining us for this unforgettable experience!'

With the exception of an obviously retired couple who looked like they'd taken a wrong turn, the other people on the tour looked as though they'd stepped out of the pages of the glossiest Instagram profiles. Most of them wore bright skinny jeans and too-clean trainers. Men and women both had perfect makeup. Jane thought of her neglected pots of foundation and mascara and wondered if she looked shabby and ordinary.

Mitch ran through a few rules about safety and emphasised the fact that photos must not be taken until they reached what he called "the facility".

'We're an open secret, but the secret part is there for a reason,' he said with a wink.

They were shepherded to a large gravel clearing which Mitch called a car park. A battered minibus awaited them. Jane checked the number plate. She was fairly certain it was from the 1970s.

'Lizzie, are you sure about this?'

Getting on a minibus in the middle of nowhere with someone who didn't want to tell you where you were going did not feel good. Even though the other tour members seemed happy enough to begin boarding the bus.

'It's fine,' said Lizzie. 'Mitch doesn't seem like an axe murderer and even if he was, he hasn't confiscated our phones. Just told us not to use them for a bit.'

'I'm pretty sure every axe murderer movie ever has the axe murderer seem not like an axe murderer.'

'Oh my God! Stop saying axe murderer!'

'Lizzie!'

'Don't worry ladies, axe murder costs extra,' said Mitch, which made Jane want to go drown herself in the loch.

Lizzie got on the bus. And despite the alarm bells ringing in her brain, Jane couldn't leave her.

***

The minibus chugged along through a thick forest. Jane sneaked a look at her phone. Three bars but no data. So she could call for help but using Google Maps to determine their location was out.

Eventually, they arrived at a building, half hidden in the undergrowth. A huge mechanical door rose up. They drove into a tunnel. Jane felt the air go stale as they got deeper. They were going underground.

When Mitch ushered them out of the bus, they were in a wide empty room, floodlit. A huge glass window stretched in front of them and above so the room was half see-through. The other side of the glass was dark with water and the muddy bed of what had to be the loch.

'And now, what you've all been waiting for!' said the tour guide. 'Here she is—Nessie!'

At first, all Jane could see was a spiral of dirt. Then she saw movement. A ripple of turquoise with scales shining in rose-gold. A chorus of awed gasps went up and everyone pressed close to the glass.

'This isn't a tank, it's a glass window built beneath the loch,' Mitch continued. 'Nessie's actual enclosure is made of wide, tangle-proof netting. Believe it or not, she's been hidden here with us since the early 1930s.'

A dozen cameras flashed as Nessie drew closer. She opened

and closed her jaw in a way that looked playful, as if she were smiling.

Jane examined the creature for strings or metal, anything that didn't look natural. When Lizzie put her hand on the glass, Nessie looked at it. Her eye was larger than the hand. She knocked her jaw against the window, as if to say hello.

'No!' said Mitch, banging on the glass. 'You know that's naughty!'

Nessie squiggled away at the noise. The guests looked perturbed and the guide sighed. 'Sorry, folks. It's just, she's got so big...'

A babble of questions went up and Mitch seemed suddenly flustered, like his worry wasn't an act.

Nessie came back to look at Lizzie again. Each one of her teeth was the size of a proper chef's knife, the ones Jane's mother said were too dangerous to own.

'She likes me,' murmured Lizzie. 'When I look at her, I can feel someone intelligent looking back. I can't explain it, but I can *feel* it.'

Jane couldn't resist taking a photo of Lizzie and Nessie looking at each other. Then she ran her hands over the glass, wondering if it could be an image on a screen, or a projection. She searched the room, but she didn't see any telltale spots of light.

Nessie seemed content to swim around for a while watching the guests, rolling over and flicking her tail. Then her mood seemed to turn sour. A slam reverberated against the glass as she whipped it with her tail. And again. And again. The lights flickered. Someone screamed.

A crack arced across the glass and water oozed in. Nessie

swam upwards in a jagged spiral until she was out of sight. Lizzie backed away, the first time Jane had even seen her look scared. An alarm began to blare.

'Out!' yelled Mitch. 'Now!'

Lizzie held her phone up so Jane could see the time. 'Seven thirty-three,' she said. 'Time for another escape attempt.'

'Yes, ours, before the room floods and we drown.'

***

They all scrambled back onto the minibus while Mitch yelled into a walkie talkie. Then he rejoined them, grim-faced and unsmiling.

'Many apologies, ladies and gentlemen. You will all receive a partial refund.'

The other guests hurried off once they were back in the car park. Their fear had turned to excitement and they seemed to accept what they'd seen as part of the experience.

'A trick with mirrors and screens,' said a girl with purple hair.

'Nah, it's animatronic,' said a male model.

Jane wanted to leave too, but Lizzie hung back. She cornered Mitch.

'Nessie's been trying to escape for a while, hasn't she? Why don't we pop into a pub and you can tell us all about it?'

Mitch went pale. 'I—I don't know what you mean...'

'The strange bubbles in the loch, around 7:30 every day? People have started to notice, you know.'

He drooped. 'I. Well. Alright. Are you journalists?'

'Private investigators,' said Lizzie. 'Sort of.'

***

There was a pub on the corner thrumming with tourists

clutching Nessie toys and wearing Nessie hats. The dinosaur-style green version so beloved by the public seemed to be everywhere. There were no turquoise eels among them, no hint at the reality behind the myth. Even the pictures on the pub's stone walls held no clues. Lizzie stood impatiently at the bar waiting to buy drinks while Jane and Mitch sat at a table shoved so far into a corner it was almost invisible.

Mitch had taken off his hat and suddenly become hand-some. Jane was still getting used to this new reality.

'I'm sorry about all this,' she managed.

'Actually, it's a relief to have someone to talk to. Everyone else is only thinking about money.'

'You must be drowning in it, the price of those tickets.'

'We do alright,' said Mitch. 'But Nessie eats a lot of it.'

'How come your Nessie's not more famous?' Lizzie demanded, banging down their first tray of beers. Jane couldn't help feeling relieved at the sight of her.

'My grandfather died last year. He ran tours for a very exclusive clientele. No scientists. No photos. But now, a lot of the usual clients have died and well...we wanted to keep the business going.'

'You've built a fortune off that poor, trapped creature,' grumbled Lizzie. 'I checked your accounts on Companies House.'

'We marketed my grandad's tours to Instagram influencers, people who splash the cash on luxury experiences. But Nessie's been different lately. Restless. Impatient. Barely eating. Banging on the glass and now...I don't know how we're going to repair it.'

'Maybe she's depressed,' said Lizzie. 'How would you feel,

stuck in a net with weird monkey people staring at you all the time?'

'Nessie *likes* people! She's usually always pleased to see you. Maybe she misses my grandad?'

'She's trying to escape! You can't keep her trapped!'

'At least she's safe. Do you know how crazy things would get if we broadcast her on the news? Scientists would all want a piece of her. Not to mention hunters and poachers and all that. It's better kept quiet, photos restricted to a select few. The rest of the world dismisses the pics as a hoax and everyone's a winner.'

'Yeah, except Nessie!'

'If she were trying to escape, where would she even go?' 'Essentially, Nessie is a bloody big eel,' said Jane. 'And all eels eventually return to the Sargasso Sea, to mate and die.'

'Since when are you an eel expert?' asked Lizzie.

'I'm not, I just like watching David Attenbrough.'

'I think maybe I should have watched it a bit more,' sighed Mitch.

'She *wants* to go,' said Lizzie. 'You know that. Deep down.'

'But to die...?'

Jane bit her lip. Perhaps she'd been cruel. Or even wrong. 'Well, regular eels. Maybe Nessie-eels are different.'

'That's not the point. The point is she wants to go,' insisted Lizzie.

'I can't just let her go,' said Mitch. 'What will I do?'

'All those books in your office,' said Jane. 'You want to travel. But you've never even left Scotland. How could you trust anyone else with Nessie? I can tell you care about her...'

'Of course I do. She's family. Ever since my grandad first took me to see her.'

'Then treat her like family and not just a wayward pet,' said Lizzie. 'She's so clever, so beautiful, so intelligent. And I think she's made her wishes very clear.'

***

Jane had never been so pleased to see such a barebones hotel room. She collapsed on one of the twin beds with an exaggerated moan of relief. Jane wanted to talk to Lizzie about everything, now they finally had room to be astonished, but somehow in her few minutes of lying down she fell dead asleep. She woke stiff in the early hours of the morning, still wearing her clothes.

She let herself drift for a while, until she heard Lizzie get up to boil the kettle for tea. Jane sat up sticky with yesterday's sweat. She really needed to shower. Lizzie poured a second cup of tea.

'I'll help you write that email to your mum, shall I? I've got that photo of you and Nessie all filtered and ready to go!'

Lizzie sighed in a great rush of breath. 'She already emailed. She sent me the details for a bank account in the name of "Busy Lizzie's Detective Agency"'.

'Oh! That's fantastic news!'

'It's a terrible name,' Lizzie grumbled, but her voice lacked the usual acid when discussing her mother. 'The money for the tour tickets should be in your account.'

A weight lifted from Jane's shoulders.

Lizzie turned and made an exaggerated thoughtful expression. 'Your moustache is looking pretty good, Watson. I wonder if you might consider joining my new agency?'

'I don't have a moustache, cheeky!'

Jane threw a pillow at her. Lizzie caught it and grinned and Jane would follow her anywhere. If she could. But...

'What's the salary then, boss?'

'...Salary?'

Jane smiled. 'Ah, well. I can't live not knowing when I'm getting paid. I think I've got to find a stable job with benefits and an office and all that.'

'But—'

'Also. As fun as this weekend's been, I've spent a lot of it scared half to death about bankruptcy, kidnapping and drowning. It's er...not such a thrill for me. Not all the time. Getting locked in the library is more my speed.'

'Alright,' said Lizzie. 'Well. I understand.'

She pulled out her phone to fiddle with, which was what she did in rare moments when she absolutely didn't know what to say. A headline flashed up on the screen. She froze and moved to sit down beside Jane, phone in one hand and teacup in the other.

They looked at the screen together.

NESSIE CAPTURED ON CAMERA AT LAST BY LO-CAL MAN! MOST CONVINCING PICTURES YET!

Lizzie tapped the notification. Below the headline was a crystal clear image of Nessie in an unmistakable, graceful leap out of the loch. Her mouth hung open in a wide grin.

An image of a very familiar man graced the screen in all his scarlet-bearded glory. Lizzie pressed play.

'I knew it! Look at her! Beautiful! I could hardly believe when she popped up on camera, I've been waiting years for this!'

'So what do you think you'll do now you've found Nessie?' asked the reporter.

'I'll keep looking for her, of course.'

'There are plenty of sceptics,' the reporter said, turning to camera. 'Scientists say the image could well be another hoax. But for some, the possibility of her existence is more than enough proof. And that possibility is the only thing important to the many tourists who visit the loch every year hoping for a glimpse of Nessie.'

'She made it,' said Lizzie, a gentle smile on her lips. 'And so will we, wherever it is we decide to swim to.'

The Special Delivery

Predicted A Level Results
Mathematics: A
Business Studies: A
Psychology: A

***

Asha took one last look, then tucked the slip of paper deep into her backpack before hitching herself onto her bike. Her mother would be excited to see her grades. The sole purpose of Asha's life for the next year was to make sure those three letters came true. She knew those letters opened the doors to universities across the country. Her mum grew excited as they travelled to Cambridge, to Sheffield, to Coventry for open days where they were laden down with leaflets.

And yet. An emptiness sat in Asha's belly. The state-of-the-art lecture theatres, the media suites filled with iMacs, the clean lines of the libraries. They held no passion, no thrill, no excitement. The thought of late nights studying or drinking too much beer did not appeal to her. In fact, the idea of the legendary Freshers' Week scared her silly.

While her friends dreamed of the societies they'd join, the

friends they'd make and even falling in love, Asha felt like she spent each day inching closer to a dark chasm. On results day, she'd get pushed in and say goodbye to everything she knew.

Auntie had just flipped the sign on *Wok This Way*'s front door to "Open" when Asha pulled up on her bike. The smell of sesame oil and fried meat spilled out. Once upon a time, it never failed to make Asha hungry. Now she was too used to it.

'Here you are,' said Auntie, clicking her tongue. Asha didn't bother locking her bike as she accepted the first load of the night and packed it into her boxy courier bag. She fired up the sat nav app on her smartphone, and then she was off.

The best thing about delivering takeaway was that people were always pleased to see you. It made all the hard pedalling, the confusing turns, the near misses with idiot drivers worth it. A smile at the door, a thanks as she handed over the bags.

As always, she lost count of how many times she went back and forth to the restaurant. Fridays were always like that. Auntie refused to let her work past 9 pm because "a young lady shouldn't be out alone". Asha had considered pressing the point, but by 9 pm she'd done four hours of cycling and was ready to collapse into bed.

The restaurant quieted in the lull between dinner and when people started pouring out of the local pub. She left Auntie manning the phone and slipped into the kitchen. It was in full *sizzle-hiss-crisp* action. Asha kept a careful eye on the fryers as she moved around them, remembering the burn of the hot oil.

Asha's dad tossed some chow mein in his favourite pan, his movements mechanical, his eyes somewhere else. As soon as he saw her though, his face changed into a gentle smile.

'Asha. Everything OK?'

'Yeah, I just wanted to say hello.'

He finished tossing the chow mein and began scooping it into plastic boxes. 'Can you do the lids?'

They worked together quietly until the noodles were boxed, sealed and ready for delivery.

'It's busy,' said Asha, as her dad loaded a new batch of noodles. She watched him expertly handle the pan and thought of the sheet of paper in her bag with the three As printed on it. Should she show him?

'How is school?' he asked, as if reading her mind. She'd given up telling him that actually it was called sixth form now.

'It's going well. We've got a new psychology teacher and I like her.'

'Good. How's your mother?'

A thornier question. Her mum and dad's divorce had sent an earthquake through her life. She remembered sitting hunched near the counter while her mum shouted things like, 'I can't remember the last time we talked without the sound of hissing oil!' Even though she lived with her mum, her dad always acted like her appearance at the takeaway was something perfectly ordinary and expected.

'She's good. She's training for a marathon.'

'She called me,' he said, which she hadn't expected. For a moment, hope flared. Perhaps they were getting back together? Perhaps her mum had woken up and realised she missed the bang-clatter of the delivery vans, the rush of customers and everything smelling like sesame?

'She said the shifts were making you tired and you need to concentrate on school.'

Asha's throat tightened and her eyes pricked with tears. 'I *want* to do the shifts. I need money for uni.'

'I have money for you, you know that.'

'I like helping you out. She can't stop me.'

He smiled, took the pan off the heat and set it down. For once she had his full attention. 'This year is really important for you. I want you to have the future you deserve.'

'If I don't come here, when will I see you?'

'Auntie says come for dinner on Monday when the restaurant is closed.'

Asha hated dinner with Auntie. She was too interested in why Asha didn't have a boyfriend yet. It was embarrassing.

'I'm not stopping my shifts. It's only two nights a week when you're busiest. I used to do much more.'

'Wouldn't you rather be out with friends on those nights?'

'I see them all day at school,' said Asha, though she wasn't sure she'd call Priti and Rebecca *friends*. More like none of them fit with any other group and so they'd ended up together, bonded by the thin thread of their school life.

'Auntie and I always appreciate your help. But we know what it's like to have life centred around making money. We didn't have a choice. You do.'

***

Asha picked up phone duty on Saturday evening. Somehow she found it even more tiring than making deliveries for four hours straight. Some of the voices were familiar, some awkward to listen to. She mixed up Fs and Ss and Ps and Ds as she struggled to find the right address on her online form.

All the while orders poured out of the kitchen ready to be bagged and picked up.

'Hello, Wok This Way. Would you like to place an order?'

'Five mooncakes please.'

Asha blinked. 'Sorry. Did you say "mooncake"?'

'Yes. Five please.'

Mooncakes were small, savoury pastries shared between friends during the Mooncake or Mid-Autumn festival. The middles were usually filled with lotus seed paste and an egg yolk to symbolise the moon.

'We're a takeaway, not a bakery.'

'Mrs Chang makes them for me.'

Asha swallowed a lump in her throat. 'I'm sorry. Mrs Chang passed away last year. You need to call a bakery.'

'What bakery?'

Her dad paused over the order he'd just deposited on the counter and signalled for the phone. Asha handed it over.

'Hello? Where would you like the mooncakes sent please?'

Her dad wrote down an address on their pad and put the phone down. Then he stared at his own writing like he couldn't believe what he'd done.

'Do we have the recipe?' said Asha, gently.

'I always meant to have another look,' said her father. 'I'm sure we must have it somewhere.'

Asha checked the address. 'London? That's a long way to send cakes.'

'I remember her baking them each year. I would like to do this for her. I'll find a way.'

***

Asha had been trying not to think about the upcoming

Mooncake festival. It wouldn't be the same without her grandmother's cooking, but she hadn't realised others would miss it too. Her grandmother always yearned to be a baker rather than a takeaway chef, but as far as Asha knew she'd never moved that dream off the ground.

It was still on her mind as she put her key in the door and let herself in.

'I'm back,' she said, before remembering her mum wasn't really talking to her since their row about her hours the previous evening. She heard the *dum-dum* of the News at 10 from the TV, so she was still up at least.

Asha peered into the living room. An empty wine bottle and pizza box were spread over the coffee table. Her mother tapped at her phone, mindlessly scrolling through Facebook photos while the TV once again spelled out the country's oncoming doom. When her mum looked up in a flick of blonde hair, her nose wrinkled at Asha's takeaway smell.

'You look tired. I'm still not happy about you working, even if it isn't on the bike.'

'I don't want this argument again.'

'Wait,' said her mother. 'Your predicted results. Why haven't you shown me? Ben showed his to Casey.'

Asha hid a grimace. She should have known.

And then a brilliant idea occurred to her.

'Here,' she said, delving into her bag and pulling out her wrinkled predictions sheet. 'And these grades were predicted for me while I was working. I really don't think it's affecting me that much.'

Her mother's eyes grew greedy when she saw the As, just as Asha knew they would.

'This gives you a shot at Cambridge,' she said and Asha swore she saw a glint of a tear in her mother's eyes. She always got like this on wine.

'Yeah,' said Asha, without enthusiasm. 'It does.'

'Asha. Don't you get it? If you give up working at the takeaway you can put everything into these grades. Do you know how competitive it is? Especially since we could never afford to put you through private schooling.'

'Mum, you're not listening. I want to help Dad too. Especially now Grandma's not around.'

Her mum sighed. She missed Asha's grandmother too.

'I *like* working at the takeaway. Why is that so hard for everyone to understand? Everything keeps changing but the takeaway is always the same. It's home.'

***

When Asha returned to *Wok This Way*, Auntie was furiously muttering as she clicked to accept online orders.

'Your father,' she said, in warning tones, 'has turned out every single box in our flat. All night I could hear him clacking around. And now there's crap everywhere!'

'Was he looking for the mooncake recipe?'

'It is sad we could never find the recipe book my mother used. We should have asked for it but everything happened so quickly...'

Asha wanted to offer Auntie comfort but she wasn't sure how. 'Why don't I help with the search?' she said. 'Or maybe I could find an online recipe?'

'Internet isn't going to replace it, but we've taken the order and must fulfil it.'

Her father's spirits seemed even lower. 'I'll make the

mooncakes tomorrow,' he said. 'That leaves me all of tonight to search. There's still time.'

'Have you slept?' Asha asked, watching his stilted movements. 'I know this is important, but is it worth the exhaustion?'

'Ah. I can't remember a time when I wasn't tired.'

'Maybe I can help.'

'Asha. You always help. But...perhaps I should ring the customer back and say we can't do it after all.'

'I want to try and make the cakes,' said Asha. 'Let's at least try.'

***

On Mondays the takeaway was closed. Everything was given a thorough deep clean until the whole building smelt of chemical solution. Asha also happened to have the day off. It was teacher training day. She imagined her teachers hunched in the classrooms, eyes glazed over as they watched PowerPoint presentations, and did not envy them.

Upstairs, in the flat above the takeaway, Asha and her father peered at pictures on her laptop screen with a critical eye.

'None of these look exactly right,' said her father. 'It feels strange trying to replace my mother's knowledge with that of a random person on the internet.'

'I know, but what else can we do?'

They'd searched all night and not found the recipe book. But Asha had found moulds to shape the cakes in, so they would at least be the right shape. She'd also found a website which offered next day delivery of ingredients that were harder to find, like lotus seeds and lye water. They had all the parts they needed. But how to assemble them?

Asha clicked on a Youtube video which made it all look like the easiest thing ever. Simply whisk this and knead that and combine this and create beautiful cakes. She knew in reality it would be much more difficult.

***

For the first batch, the dough didn't come together and the cakes cracked in the oven. The second batch somehow had soggy pastry. The third came out slightly wonky where Asha pressed too hard on the moulds. The empty egg boxes were beginning to stack up in the recycling.

By batch four, Asha's mood had sagged but her father kept on going, still eager. Cooking the same food six nights a week gave him a legendary amount of patience.

And finally, they had the perfect cakes. Beautiful golden pastry and a savoury-sweet middle.

'Not anywhere close to my mother's, but perfectly edible,' said her father.

They got Auntie to taste test for them and she agreed with the assessment. The mooncakes were perfectly adequate.

Now the only thing left to do was make the delivery.

'Just a couple of hours on the train into London and then a short hop on the Underground. It isn't too bad,' said Asha. Her mother often took her into the city for the theatre or the museums. She'd done the trip a few times.

When they saw how much the tickets were, her father and auntie exchanged panicked looks. They'd already spent a lot on ingredients. Profits from the takeaway were narrow.

'Why don't I go by myself?' said Asha. 'I've got a railcard

and I've done it loads of times. I can pay for the ticket out of my savings.'

They argued for a few minutes. Asha pointed out a) she did unsupervised deliveries every day, b) she was going to an extremely busy area of the city in daylight hours and c) she was extremely reliable, sensible and careful and if they wished to dispute this she might not forgive them.

She was allowed to go, on the condition that her mother agreed.

'Nothing I say is going to stop you, is it?' her mother asked over the phone. She was still at work.

'No.'

'Keep in touch via text. As soon as I don't get a response I'm calling the police.'

A bit much, but it was the best Asha was going to get.

***

Asha wheeled her bike off the train, mooncakes carefully packed into her bulky courier's bag. She dashed off a text to let her parents know she'd arrived without incident.

The station thrummed with passengers. Asha wrestled the bike through the barriers under the pitying eye of a guard. She decided then and there she wouldn't bother with the Underground—there were perfectly good cycle paths leading to where she needed to go. She donned her helmet and took to the road.

Drivers in London were absolutely mental. This was a land of no patience and no indicators. The taxis barrelling about were intimidating but she kept to her route, watching the minutes to her destination tick ever downwards on her app.

Twenty minutes of harrowing road riding and she reached

a terraced street buried between cafes, barbers and super-markets. The houses were three-storied with bay windows which looked as if they'd been standing since before Asha was born. The air felt thick with history.

She located the right number, 15, and pressed the buzzer for Flat 2. Out of habit, she took off her bag and unzipped the lid, ready to hand the cakes over.

After a couple of minutes, the scuffle of a key alerted her to someone opening the door.

The gentleman gave her an inquiring head tilt, until he spotted the mooncakes. Then he grinned so hard she could see where he was missing two molars.

He greeted her in Cantonese. When he heard her clumsy—but hopefully correct—response, he switched to English.

'Hello, young lady. Right on time.'

'These mooncakes—they weren't made by Mrs Chang. But I hoped you might accept these with our best wishes, as my father recalled her making these every year.'

He took the box from her bag and flipped it open to inspect them. 'They look lovely,' he paused. 'A good job, as I have some hungry ghosts to feed.'

He laughed. What a strange gentleman.

'Something else,' he added. 'Mrs Chang said to tell you to look on the right of the counter as you come in and put your hand next to the wall, right near the bottom.'

Asha blinked. 'What? When...?'

'That's what she said,' he insisted. 'Mrs Chang is not a lady you easily forget.'

'Touch the wall on the right of the counter, near the bottom,' she repeated.

'It seemed important to her,' said the gentleman.

A door slammed in the house behind him. A strange whistle started up, like a queasy kettle.

'I must go, it's feeding time. Thank you for the cakes and take care, young lady.'

Before she could ask any more questions, he shut the heavy door. As she left, she felt eyes on her. When she looked up at the house, she saw a figure at the window, waving at her. A blink later and it was gone.

Asha was very tired. She must have been seeing things.

She texted her parents to let them know she was on her way home. The train journey left her fidgety and restless. Her mother had told her to go home, but she couldn't wait another night.

***

When she got to the takeaway, it was dark.

'Your mother will be worried,' her father said. 'Have you eaten?'

Asha had forgotten about food. Her mind was only on one thing.

Asha crouched down under the counter on the right and felt for the wedge of space between the plasterboard and the wall. At first she could feel only rough brick. She pushed her hand further in and then she felt the brush of paper against her skin. Gently, she grasped for the edge of it.

'Asha, what are you doing down there?'

She didn't answer. Her heart beat hard. She pictured her grandmother standing over the oven, impatiently watching the timer. The smell of fresh pastry. The handwritten recipe book on the counter, splattered with sugar and melted butter.

Please let this be it.

She shuffled the book back against the wall and pulled it through the gap. She saw a splash of blossom print and her grandmother's neat Cantonese. She'd found it. The insides were crammed with the same hand, the letters in red, black or blue biro.

Asha scrambled to her feet and held out the recipe book. 'It was here all along.'

Her father took the book. Flicked the cover open. Loose leaf pages, yellowed with age, stuck out from the sides.

'How did you know where to look?'

'The man in London told me. He was strange. He said he had to feed some hungry ghosts.'

Neither of them could come up with a rational explanation. Even Auntie didn't remember him coming into the restaurant and she had a mind like a steel trap. His name and address weren't on file even though he'd bought mooncakes from them for years.

'An explanation will come along when we've stopped looking for one,' said Auntie. 'Hungry ghosts was probably a joke about the festival.'

'Here are the mooncakes,' said her father, stopping at a page with a gorgeous hand drawn diagram of the layers.

Seeing the picture made something fall into place for Asha. She knew what she wanted to do after A Levels. Now she just had to convince everyone else, starting with her mother.

***

Asha carefully unbundled the leftover mooncakes Auntie had packed up for her. She was exhausted, but excited too.

Like she'd been stuck on a frustrating maths problem for a long time and had finally stumbled on the solution.

Asha watched her mum sample a moon cake. 'Mmm. These are good.'

Asha took a deep breath.

'I've made a decision. I want to study to become a chef. I know it's long hours and hard work but it's what I want. Making these cakes showed me what I can do. One day I want to run the takeaway in my own way. Like, maybe we could add a bakery.'

'Asha. Slow down. I hear what you're saying but...maybe give it a week. See if that's what you really want. I know how often things change at your age.'

Asha nodded. 'And if I don't change my mind?'

'If you spend three years studying something you don't want, it'll leave you frustrated. I wouldn't want you to waste your time like that.'

Asha smiled. She bit into a mooncake and thought of the future. Her old anxiety had faded, replaced by a bubbling excitement, her mind aglow with possibilities.

Finally, she'd found the purpose she'd been searching for.

The Light of the Lantern

'Thanks so much for this,' said Annika.

Bella stuck her tongue out in that stupid dog way everybody else thinks is cute. Before I knew it she was sprawled in the boot of my car along with a basket, several packets of dog treats, an assortment of toys and a lead. I spotted a tuft of black fur stuck to the leather interior and tried not to mind.

I really didn't want to take Bella home with me. But neither did I want my sister to miss out on the last minute trip to Rome her boyfriend had booked for their anniversary. My six-year-old nephew Jonas was going to our mum's, but she didn't have the room—or patience—for the dog. I didn't blame her.

Jonas started crying.

'Bella's going to have a holiday, just like you. She'll be fine,' I assured him.

'But what if she gets lost and doesn't remember the way home?' he wailed.

I'm a man of forty-one. We're not supposed to have feelings to hurt, so I ignored his insinuation I was useless enough to lose one very large, very black dog.

'I won't lose her, mate. Promise.'

'You will be alright, won't you?' Annika fussed. 'You will call me if anything goes wrong?'

'For goodness sake Ann, I'm not an idiot,' I snapped. She held her hands up in a placating gesture, but not before I saw her flinch. Then I felt guilty.

'Don't worry. Just go and enjoy the attentions of your fancy new fella. The world won't cave in because you're going on holiday.'

Bella tried to lick me. I pushed her off. It was important to set boundaries and I wasn't falling for the cute act. One of Annika's care notes, from her painstakingly formatted email, read "Will try and murder rabbits, DO NOT LET HER EAT THEM."

Other choice selections included "Needs long walkies once a day, short walkies once a day" and "Keep on lead unless certain no other small furry animals within a one-mile radius". Being ignorant in the ways of dog ownership, I didn't see anything particularly unusual about these directions.

Maybe I should have.

***

Twenty years ago my flat had been freshly painted and the carpets were always immaculate because my ex-wife had an obsession with vacuuming. Now it was obvious I rarely received guests. A week's worth of washing up sat in the sink. Laundry festered in random piles—I didn't have enough baskets to hold my backlog. The stark white walls contrasted nicely with the clutter of my existence. I switched the kettle on, as was my habit when returning from the Great World Beyond My Flat. I wanted to read Annika's notes again, carefully, to make sure I hadn't missed anything. I rinsed my favourite mug out, ready to fill with a good old builder's brew.

Bella, bored already, tipped the bin over in one effortless sweep of her paws.

'No!' I said in my fiercest voice. I was determined to be the best temporary dog-owner ever and that meant not letting her scoff anything but the finest Pedigree chum.

Bella didn't even look at me as she gobbled the remains of my Greggs meal deal. So I needed to empty the bins. Understood.

I dragged her away with a few firm tugs at the collar, careful not to hurt her. She turned to look at me then, all innocent eyes, and let me take her down the hallway. The flat had two bedrooms. The second one was too small to be useful for much anymore, but for this weekend at least it would serve a purpose.

'This is going to be your room,' I told her, pushing open the door to the second bedroom's plain, white emptiness. I wondered why I was talking to her and surmised it was because that's what people did on TV.

I'd planned to put the dog bed in the room, along with all the other bits from the car. If I did a good job looking after Bella, maybe Annika would trust me with Jonas instead of wasting so much money on sitters. I'd imagined sending her a cute pic of Bella tucked happily into bed so she could see we were fine.

Bella had other ideas. She started barking as soon as I ushered her inside. Not playfully, but with a growling menace.

'Hush,' I pleaded with Bella, worried about disturbing the neighbours on my right, who were retired and liked nothing more than to post passive-aggressive notes through my letterbox.

Bella wouldn't hush. Her eyes bulged and then she howled, like a wolf, at the top of her voice. She launched herself at me, jaw snapping. I ducked, tripped over my own feet and hurtled to the ground. I heard the metal clasp on Bella's collar rattle as she ran back down the hall and into the kitchen.

I stayed on the floor, shocked, carpet pressed into my cheek. OK. Let the stupid dog kill herself by eating plastic milk cartons if she wants to. Then I thought about the look on Jonas's face if anything happened to his beloved pet and dragged myself upright.

The air in the room was stale from being shut up so long. It was mostly empty—just a few boxes I couldn't bear to get rid of. They covered the marks the cot made on the carpet, though I could never forget they were there. Funny how a life only eleven months long could leave such a heavy, tiny foot-print. I often thought about my son and wondered if there was a parallel world out there where we might be celebrating his twenty-first birthday. A world where I had seen his first words, his first day at school. A world where I met his first girlfriend and taught him to drive. I couldn't stop wishing myself into that parallel world, pointless though it was.

In the kitchen, something smashed against the tiles. I knew without checking it was my favourite mug. Damn dog.

* * *

Bella was bouncing off the walls after her ill-gotten meal, so I took her out.

A big dog like Bella needs to run around like a maniac at least once a day. I drove her on to the fens, as Annika instructed. It was the nearest place with space enough for her to really run. We called a truce over a game of fetch. I used a plastic scoop thing so I could keep throwing the ball without wrecking my back. I don't know why Bella found it so fun, but at least she seemed happy. I had finally become decent at dog sitting, so I savoured sweet victory.

There were a few signs about keeping dogs under close control, but I wasn't worried. As long as I threw the ball, Bella looked at me like I was a god.

My surroundings were flat plains of green-brown, interspersed with reedbeds and grey lakes. No diving, said the signs, as if it were even a little bit tempting. Birds flocked in huge numbers, flapping and honking. Reeds came right over my head, seven feet tall. The stalks were thick and golden and went on for miles around stretches of murky water.

This might sound pleasant, but in early spring the air quickly turned to freezing fog. And it was impossible not to end up mired in slippery mud, try as you might to hop-scotch round it. You could even taste mud in your breath. The thought of doing the walk again tomorrow instilled a firm sense of dread. I stared at a lone, dead tree with jagged wood sticking up from its trunk.

My phone started buzzing, a twenty-first century noise in an ancient soundscape.

'How badly do you want to kill me?' asked Annika as soon as I picked up.

'You'd better hope you're out of the country.'

She laughed. 'We're waiting in the pub until we're called for departure. I can run back if you really want me to. Last chance.'

'No, you can't!' said her boyfriend. 'Hello again!'

'Hi!' I said, rolling my eyes. 'There is one tiny thing: Bella won't go in the spare room. I put her bed in there but she just howls and barks until I let her go somewhere else.'

'Let her go somewhere else, then,' said Annika. 'She's funny like that. Kind of...special.'

'What doesn't she like? White walls? Beige carpets? Boxes? I really don't know where else to put her.'

'It's complicated. She's not like other dogs.'

'Everyone says that about their dog.'

'She's sensitive, alright? Probably something to do with the bastard who abandoned her in the fens. It's probably too small for her, that's all. Put her dog bed somewhere else.'

'Fine. It's only for a couple of days. You owe me, Annika.'

'I really do! How about I help you clear out that old room sometime, hmm?'

'...Yeah. Maybe.'

'Well, if you want to take Jonas more in the future he's going to need somewhere to sleep! See you soon!'

'Travel safe!'

I clicked off the call, my heart light at the mention of Jonas. Annika deserved someone nice who would spoil her, someone prepared to take on both Jonas and a mad dog just so they could have a future together. I knew she'd had it rough in her divorce, which we'd bonded over, but she'd come out the other side with a shining future.

The same couldn't be said for me. Annika had always been the one born under a luckier star. Sometimes it was hard not to resent it. My own divorce years earlier had been spiky and ugly. The spectre of my dead child swung the sickle down on the marriage with brutal finesse.

Then I noticed Bella was gone. No barking. No swish of black fur. I scooped her ball up again. Maybe the sound of it being thrown would summon her from whatever exciting thing she'd run off towards.

I urged myself to keep calm. I couldn't have lost a huge, black dog. No way. I yelled myself hoarse for a while. Then I remembered something Annika said about whistling. On my second whistle, Bella barked.

She'd wandered off the trail, that was all. I shoved my way through the reeds until I could see her. Bella stood shoulder-deep in a brown, crescent-shaped pool.

'Fetch, then,' I said impatiently. 'Where's the ball?'

She tilted her head and whined before barking.

'You're stuck, are you? Fine. Stay there.'

I searched for a route through the reeds but it seemed I was going to have to get in the water. An unpleasant trickle of sloppy mud filled my wellies as soon as I stepped in.

Bella took off like a rocket in the direction I'd come from, barking joyfully. Definitely laughter, I thought, especially after she thoroughly splashed me. I'd got myself wet for nothing. I had the feeling Bella had known exactly where she'd been going and what she'd been doing, and I'd been thoroughly played.

As I extracted myself from the water, Bella's ball came hurtling towards me. I jumped as it dropped at my feet. In the distance was a shining light. It was too bright for me to make out anything but a blurry figure beyond it. A birdwatcher?

'Thanks!' I yelled, holding my hand up in a wave.

I saw Bella sat at the figure's feet having her head petted, good as gold. Typical.

I turned away and threw the ball, hoping Bella would follow me back to the car.

Mercifully, she did.

***

The next day I woke groggy from half-remembered dreams. Meanwhile Bella had eaten most of my sofa. I decided it was fair to ask Annika to pay for a replacement.

I thought about tidying up, but today a new melancholy hit me. As I stood in the baby's room, I couldn't stop thinking about how it should be a proper room by now, with a bed and a computer and piles of comic books. Maybe spaceships on the wall, like Jonas had. I was back in my parallel universe, the sharp-warm pain of it. I needed to get out, but I could never close the door behind me.

My life was fine, I told myself. I was only missing a gym membership, an electric car, a partner to share my bed at night. Maybe if I found one or all of them I'd be fine. As I slopped dog food into a bowl, I knew I definitely wasn't missing having a dog. All my suspicions about them being smelly, slobbery and barky were true. There was something else weird about Bella though. Something sinister underneath the daft dog act...

The letter box clanked with today's post. Bella skidded on the kitchen tiles before falling head over tail in her eagerness to eat the mail. OK. Maybe "sinister" was a stretch and I was assigning broader intelligence where none existed.

***

'No running off today,' I warned Bella. I felt like she understood me perfectly.

I wanted to take the trail which favoured open grassland, so I could keep a close eye on her. Her black fur stood out where everything washed together in a haze of grey-green-brown. The fens were no more welcoming than the previous day, so watery the landscape seemed to blur into one big smear. The freezing air leeched any warmth from my bones. I wanted to get out of there as soon as possible.

'Hello! Nice day, isn't it!' said a woman in a thick raincoat. She had one of those tiny toy dogs. Too much fur and too little brain, if you ask me. I remembered Annika's instructions about not letting Bella off the lead around anything small and furry.

Bella snapped her jaws in a growl.

'Don't worry, mine is friendly,' said the woman.

'Mine isn't,' I sighed. 'I think she misses my sister. I'm dog sitting, see?'

'Dogs can sense emotions, you know. When you're scared or upset, she'll think there's a threat and start acting up.'

I nodded politely, wondering how to tell her Bella *liked* upsetting me. But a man being bullied by a dog is ridiculous, so I kept my mouth closed and kept my grip tight as Bella seemed very intent on lurching towards the other dog and devouring it. Annika had not exaggerated in her notes.

Bella's tugs on the lead were so insistent I had no choice but to follow her. She was not interested in open grassland of course, but led me back into the reeds. It seemed she was on familiar ground as she wove through, trampling anything in her way. Our journey was marked by the sound of wings flapping. It seemed no bird wanted to stay in our path. The ever-present squawking and honking faded to silence.

Once I deemed us far enough away from the other dog, I unclipped Bella's lead. Then I flexed my aching shoulder. She hadn't been gentle in her pulling.

I didn't know where we were but I assumed we would come back to the main path at some point if I started to loop back. Bella looked at me expectantly. I threw the ball. At this point I knew I was her slave and could do nothing about it.

One of my throws was sloppy and sent the ball careening into the reeds. Bella went after it. She did not return.

I whistled. The air remained still. The silence was unnerving and it was getting dark. But I couldn't leave Bella lost. I thought of Jonas, the look on his face as he waved us goodbye. I sighed and stepped into the reeds, shoving my way through with brute force. The brown muddy crescent lake appeared again. This was all very familiar from yesterday. I searched for what Bella might find so fascinating about this place.

Then I saw a light and a figure. I remembered Bella sat at its feet the previous day.

'Hello!' I shouted. 'Have you seen my dog? I think you rescued her ball yesterday?'

I got close enough to see the figure was a man. He turned from me and walked on, carrying the light. It wasn't a torch, but something iron-wrought, old fashioned. A lantern. I couldn't see Bella.

'Excuse me, mate,' I said, running to catch up. 'I don't suppose you know the way back to the car park, do you?'

I peered at the man's face in the lantern light. It looked

like his features had been painted slightly off kilter, but I couldn't look away. At last he spoke.

'You found my dog. Thank you.'

His voice was deep and smooth. He must have been twenty-one years old. Strong and handsome. He had Annika's freckles and my eyebrows. My blood stopped. It couldn't be. I refused to believe it.

The lantern man threw Bella's ball. She barked, shooting out of the reedbed from places unknown. Maybe she'd somehow understood I needed rescuing from my own delusions. But she ignored me and ran to the strange man. She jumped up and licked his face with aggressive enthusiasm. I'd never seen her behave like that around even Jonas. Her tail wagged so hard I thought it might fall off.

The man addressed me, surprisingly gentle.

'Dad. It's alright. It really is me. I came back to find you.'

I already knew. There was enough of me reflected in his face to trigger an instinctive recognition, the kind only a parent would feel. I never heard his first words, saw his first steps or picked him up from school. Yet there was my son. He couldn't be anyone else. I had somehow made my way into the parallel world of my waking dreams. I wanted to stay in it.

'Look at the light,' he ordered. 'And come with me.'

The more I looked, the more my frantic emotions dulled. I accepted the lantern from his hand and followed him as he walked further still into the dark and wet. Reeds bunched around me and soon I couldn't move without them brushing my clothes, my cheeks.

'Where are we going?' I asked. He didn't reply.

Then I wasn't only in the reeds, but in water. My wellies

got stuck, but I couldn't bring myself to care. The only place I wanted to be was wherever my son was going. Bella ran at his heels. The familiar way they moved together suggested owner and master.

I caught another glimpse of his face but this time it was white and hollow, with only a suggestion of a nose, a mouth. A ghoul's visage.

When someone wants to see a ghost, it makes things so much easier.

The words weren't spoken aloud. I heard them in my bones. I stared into the light of the lantern as I felt myself sink. The sky was getting further away, the reeds getting taller. Water closed over my head, mud filled my nostrils.

Bella looked down at me from the reedbed, tongue stuck out in that stupid doggy way everyone else thinks is cute.

The Cold Cowboy

I haunt my flat, trailing from room to room wondering where I've left my keys, or why I thought the kitchen counter was a good place to keep deodorant. Yesterday's clothes are flung on the sofa, my backpack is somehow in the fridge. Perhaps if I just put everything on the floor, I'd stop losing things. My keys are in the sink. Why?

I obviously know that things are where I left them when I was too tired to worry about finding them the next day. Serious message to my past and future self—you have a hook bought and hammered into the wall specifically for not losing your keys—bloody use it!

If I miss the bus I will be late for work. Then Marion will ask me if everything is alright and I will deck her in her pruney face and be at the Job Centre by 10 am. Or the police station. This chain of events strikes me as amusing. If everyone at the Job Centre didn't loathe me to my bones, I might do it. Poor old Margery and Thomas and Jim are long tired of my shenanigans. Their disappointed faces had once been entertaining, but we were all too tired of each other for further confrontation to hold any amusement.

The bus stops, three minutes late. The driver grunts an

affirmation at my request for a return ticket and indicates the card reader. I wave my card and yank the ticket too hard, so the whole reel comes spinning out. The driver throws me a filthy look. I go wide-eyed and innocent. He clacks around with the machine while I take a seat and flick through my blank bus tickets. I pull out a chewed-up biro and ink destinations on them. *Loserville, the Hell Mouth, the Shadow Realm, the Void, Victoria Rail Station.* It's something to do while we trundle along. I wonder how many hours I've spent on this bus, trying to while the minutes away. Life is one long routine, trawling from place to place; eating, working, splashing cash on entertainments to ease the boredom. There's comfort and familiarity in it, but it makes time disappear all too quickly.

***

The restaurant-slash-bar I work at is called George's Saloon and themed after my boss's favourite movies, which all take place in the Wild West. We all wear cowboy hats. The tables are decorated with knitted cacti and nodding cows. There is buffalo print wallpaper, which everybody hates because whatever you are doing, a buffalo is watching you.

George thinks the punters love it, but what they really love (although *love* might be a strong word) is Marion's cooking. Marion knows this and as a consequence she acts like she owns the place. Although, to be fair, if she didn't, the place would have closed down ages ago. George doesn't seem to grasp the concept of normal work things like fire safety and payroll. He almost agreed my pay would be fifty quid an hour before she stepped in. I linger in the cloak room and stick a ticket for the *Hell Mouth* in Marion's coat pocket. It's a thoughtful gesture really. She might be homesick.

I put my cowboy hat on and take a breath before going in properly.

'Morning, pardner,' says Ashlyn. She is George's favourite because she also likes cowboy movies. I have left a ticket for *Loserville* in her coat pocket.

It's not that I have a particular dislike of Ashlyn, I just find her terribly dull. On one particularly slow afternoon, I fashioned all the nodding cows little hats out of torn up napkins while she flicked through one of those girly magazines about makeup and self-empowerment.

'Why did you put hats on them?' she fussed when she looked up. 'They'll only fall off when they nod.'

'I thought their ears looked cold.'

Granted, my sense of humour isn't for everyone. But most people would have at least cracked a smile.

We clean the bar and all the tables. Marion cooks breakfasts, making the place smell like baked beans and bacon. George assures the customers this is authentically cowboy. They look at him like he's mad, which he is. Opening a cowboy-themed restaurant in a classically English market town is an extremely questionable life choice. Many locals complain the saloon-style storefront with its obnoxious lettering spoils the town's "character". I always wonder what character they're talking about. To me it seems perpetually damp with pot-holed roads and the same five shops you can find anywhere. There's one decent pub not run by a chain. I've been barred from it for stealing too many pint glasses.

***

George's Saloon has a slow trickle of customers, never the heaving crowds George is hoping for, especially not on a Saturday when everyone legs it to a proper town. At 2 pm, after George is sure no one else is going to show up for lunch, he calls the four of us for a meeting. He wants to discuss marketing. These meetings are never productive.

'You young people!' he says, pointing at me and Ashlyn. 'I need you to make the Saloon go viral on the TikTok. Then we'll get hundreds through the door.'

Last time it was YouTube. The time before that it was "tweeter". I expect next time we'll be begging for customers on LinkedIn. I'm tempted to suggest MySpace. George would probably go for it.

'Sure,' said Ashlyn. 'I mean, we can try.' She shoots me a wary glance, already knowing not to count on too much help from me.

Marion nods. 'Ash can film me cooking. If we show people the food is delicious, they'll come.'

I actually like Marion's cooking, her fry-ups are unrivalled, but the presentation isn't pretty enough for people to post it all over social media with cute hashtags.

George nods. 'An excellent idea. Let's get to it!'

'It won't work,' I say, point blank. Three frosty gazes turn my way. 'Look. The food we have isn't special enough to sell coming here. We need something else. We need a story.'

'Excuse you, nothing special,' Marion sniffs.

'Yes, I won't hear a bad word against Marion's cooking,' George puts in.

'I never said the cooking was bad. I said it wasn't *special.*

Like, English breakfast and burgers and chips you can get pretty much anywhere.'

They know I'm right. They still hate me. I press on. There is nowhere I am more comfortable than thin ice.

'If we want to sell this place, we need a story.' I turn to George. 'Could any of your family have been cowboys?'

'My mother was Polish and my father's from Sunderland.'

'Yes, alright, but before that.'

'No.'

'Look, it doesn't have to be *true*.'

'So what if it were?' says Marion. 'I would say most of the town is dubious or disparaging of cowboys, so they won't care if George is actually a blood-born cowboy or whatever you're going for.'

'How can you not love cowboys?' George cries. 'Miserable buggers, all of them!'

'They might well be miserable buggers, but if they don't come in and buy our food, we've had it. Not to alarm anyone, but there needs to be much less red in the account books if we're to survive the year.'

Marion is right. It's an idea but not *the* idea. They start to faff about with Ashlyn's phone in the kitchen while George narrates. So I leave them to their fruitless TikTok-ing and slope off for my break.

I know how it is. I'm the new guy, not quite one of the gang. I've done all the cleaning and taking orders and mixing drinks stuff, but I don't fit. Different place, same old story.

***

It's not market day, so a lap of the town takes about ten minutes.

I dither about buying a sausage roll and a mediocre coffee. I choose the bench in the town square least splattered with pigeon muck and contemplate my future. I see a green and yellow sign. I see tight-lipped Margery making me fill in more forms. Can I really be bothered with all that Job Centre nonsense again?

'Hello again,' I say to my favourite pigeon. 'My day has been mediocre so far, thank you for asking.'

A tour group catches my eye. I recognise the guide from my school days. His name used to be Charles but these days he goes by Sabre. He's wearing a top hat with steampunk goggles. Every time he moves, the various gears and chains strung into his clothing clink.

He stands in front of the old town hall with its ever-crumbling roof. Every year the town begs for donations for the roof and every year they continue not to fix it.

'This of course, is where the town's most famous ghoul hails from. The former stable boy's cries of "I'm cold" can still be heard on dark, misty nights—'

Sabre catches my eye. We are not friends, but have shared trauma related to the hell that was high school PE lessons. I raise a hand in acknowledgement and he nods, like one of the cows in the Saloon. He's always been a socially awkward sort of guy, not someone I thought would be comfortable standing in front of a crowd telling ghost stories.

He continues droning on about the ghost of the cold stable boy. I've never seen anything resembling a crowd in this town before, but this lot seem to be hanging on Sabre's every word. So cowboys are a no, but ghosts a yes? I am sure this says something unflattering about the psyche of my fellow residents.

Maybe I should suggest changing the restaurant to be ghost-themed. We could wear pumpkins on our heads instead of cowboy hats.

I instantly dismiss even suggesting it. George would never go for it.

I consider sodding off home. It's not like there'll be any customers at the Saloon.

But even the thought of my cold, cluttered flat points my feet straight back towards the restaurant. At least in there, George will talk my ear off about running cowboy film nights or buying decorative cacti. Marion might let me have another go with the grillpan, as long as she keeps an eye on anything flammable. Ashlyn will have another magazine quiz we could do about "How to spend your hot girl summer" or some such nonsense.

Caring about people is a lot of effort. I decided a while ago not to bother, save myself the hassle. And what do I care about some silly restaurant? They all drive me nuts. And I drive them nuts. I definitely don't care about what happens to George's life savings or Marion's mortgage or Ashlyn's wedding plans.

All the same, an idea begins to form in my mind.

***

The video making in the Saloon goes on. I serve a few people milkshakes. We make them with chunks of Milky Bar...because there's a cowboy on the packet. No other reason.

Usually I'm off like a shot to get back on my bus as soon

as the place closes, but tonight I linger. George is still in his office. I can hear nasally shouting and gunshots blasting out from the massive TV he has in there. Marion gives me a sceptical look on the way out as I pretend to clean a spotless table.

As soon as she's gone, I step into the kitchen. I roll up my sleeves and get to work.

I dump flour all over the worktops, making white snowdrifts, leaving clouds of it filling the still, quiet air. There are twenty-four eggs, which I delight in hurling at random spots on the wall. I pull out the freezer drawers and rearrange them. Same with Marion's neatly ordered spice rack.

On the largest worktop, I press my index finger into the flour and write a note.

Then I fill the sink with water until it's overflowing, erasing my floury footprints.

I hear footsteps. It must be George, getting ready to go home. A delicious buzz of adrenaline courses through me. Booking it out of a window is nostalgic; it reminds me of living with my parents.

***

I let myself into my dark flat. My life motto, stolen from a long-ago internet meme: I'm looking for trouble and if I cannot find it, I will create it. I abandon my things wherever, uncaring about tomorrow morning. Poltergeists don't fear confusion, they thrive on it.

I can turn all the lights on in the flat, I can toss things about, I can turn up the volume on the TV until the walls vibrate. It still feels devoid of colour, of character, of life.

My girlfriend left me a year ago, fed up with trying to bail me out of my latest drama. There are still empty spaces where she used to stash her shoes and hang her coat. I sometimes miss the heels and the boots and the trainers cluttering up my hallway.

I've never been able to handle the itch of chaos crawling under my skin. My ex thought she could change me and she was wrong. Every job I get thinks they can make me into a neat little worker drone and they're wrong too.

The thrill is in the moment, when you're doing exactly what you want and it's a terrible idea. Not even the dread afterwards can touch it. Makes a man feel alive.

***

'Office,' Marion says as soon as I appear at work the next day. 'Now.'

'You don't have an office.'

Marion rolls her eyes. 'George's office. Obviously.'

This talk is only going to end one way. Job Centre, here I come. Whatever, I don't care.

We sit down. I pick up George's dancing cactus toy and set it off merrily line dancing. Marion waits patiently for the cactus to shut up. I wonder if this is how her conversations with George go as well.

'Funny,' she says once it's quiet, waving her ticket for the *Hell Mouth* at me.

I keep my face carefully blank.

'I know it was you. I've seen your handwriting on the customer feedback cards. We got six in a row saying "Rob is an angel and deserves a raise". Might want to think about spacing them out next time.'

'Worth a shot.'

'Not everyone finds these amusing, you know,' she says, holding up her ticket. 'Ashlyn was quite upset.'

'Poor Ashlyn,' I say, extremely insincere.

'You'll need to apologise to her. You know, you don't have to work here if it's not for you. You could go somewhere else.'

'I've *been* everywhere else.'

I have been around several bars, worked in the post office, Poundland and Tesco. I lasted no more than a week at each. I have been at George's Saloon for eighteen days, which is a record.

'OK,' says Marion. 'Then what do you want to do? Because at this rate, you're not going to pass probation here either. Mind you, if the poor custom keeps up we might all find ourselves down the Job Centre with you.'

No one's ever asked me what I *want* to do. I have no idea what to say to her. So I deflect, like I always do.

'I want to be a TikTok sensation.'

She snorts. 'No. Come on. Be serious.'

'I don't know,' I mumble.

It's much easier to know what you *don't* want to do, which is everything else I've tried so far. George's Saloon isn't the worst place I've worked, not by a long shot.

I am saved from further interrogation by George barging in. 'Marion! Have you seen the state of the kitchen?'

***

One of the layabout officers from the local police station stands in the messy kitchen, looking bored. 'A practical joker, no doubt,' she says. 'Any serious property damage? Or theft?'

Marion shakes her head. 'They didn't take anything. George's safe hasn't been touched. Nor his computer.'

George's computer is twelve years old and it takes fifteen minutes to load a Google search. Anyone stealing that would live to regret it.

The officer narrows her eyes at me. 'I know you,' she says.

I shake my head. 'No, we've never met.'

'Really? I'm seeing a horse. On the school roof. And wasn't there a fire, during a chemistry lesson—'

'Oh no, that was my friend. People say we could be twins.'

'Hmm.'

'I was the last one out of here,' George says. 'Place was empty when I left.'

'It was a ghost,' wails Ashlyn. 'It must have been. Just look at the message!'

The officer sighs. 'Right. Of course. I'll just ring up Scooby Doo, shall I?'

'That would be lovely, cheers,' says George.

***

We do not get Scooby Doo. We get Sabre, who rattles in as soon as we open. I've never seen him so animated. He's holding a camera with a massive lens and a little black circular device that makes weird, random crackles.

'It's for sensing phantasmic energy,' he explains.

George and Marion are dubious, but Sabre is all too excited to beetle around the kitchen. I have never seen a person vibrate with excitement before, but he's utterly, completely delighted.

He snaps several pictures of the floury worktop and its ominous message: "Yee-hah! I'm cold."

Look. I did my best and I have seen far fewer cowboy movies than George considers ideal.

'Seeing this message, there is no doubt in my mind,' Sabre says with more dramatic flair than I can ever remember him having. 'You were visited by the stable boy's ghost. The very same one that's haunted the town for years. And what's more...it seems he was not just a stable boy but a *cowboy*! An immigrant! What a wonderful twist in the tale!'

George blinks. 'Er, right. And that's good?'

'It's amazing,' enthuses Sabre. 'All my online friends are going to be *so jealous* of my—I mean *your* discovery.'

***

I haven't sat down in three hours. The Saloon is filled with ghost hunters gawping at the buffalo wallpaper and making the cows on the tables nod-nod-nod. I almost regret my good deed. Especially after Marion had me scraping egg off the wall for what felt like hours.

'I don't believe in ghosts,' Marion tells me while I wait for her to load up the next burger plates. I'm slightly breathless and I shrug, desperate to get away.

'If it wasn't a ghost,' she continues, 'someone *did* break in. But they didn't nick the hundreds of pounds worth of equipment. In fact, they seemed to carefully avoid damaging it. Which is odd, don't you think?'

'Maybe they didn't know what any of it was.'

'No, I think they knew exactly what they were doing. And they especially knew what they were doing when they called their good old school buddy ghost enthusiast afterwards.'

She raises a meaningful eyebrow while I shift from foot to foot. I wilt. God, she's good.

'Have you told George um...anything?'

'George is having a lovely time chatting with the local paper about the revelation that the town's most famous ghost is apparently a cowboy. I suppose the "ghost" will either have to own up and face the music...or never receive credit for their bonkers yet brilliant marketing strategy.'

'Mmm-hmm.'

Marion bursts out laughing. '"Yee-hah! I'm cold!" Really, Rob? You could have written something scarier than that.'

'The Wild West is much warmer, no wonder the poor ghost is cold.'

'Right. Well, the ethics of hijacking a donkey-year-old ghost story for our own purposes are perhaps slightly dubious.'

'Every story is another story told again. Stories don't belong to anyone.'

Marion finishes the plates. 'Well. I reckon this story is going to pay off my mortgage.'

'So—'

'So I'm going to recommend to George that you pass probation. We need the extra help and can't waste time training anyone new. But I'm watching you. Touch my kitchen again and you'll wish you really were a ghost.'

I make my escape. More customers come in, so I regale them with the tale of the cowboy ghost. Ashlyn blends milkshakes. A gang of teens point their phones around the place, examining the cacti and choosing their favourite buffalo on the wallpaper.

It beats the Job Centre. Perhaps I'll do my best to stay a while.

The Quickest Way to Fix
a Printer

Amy waited next to the printer. She was one of those glamorous women who made jokes about wine o'clock and made me want to hide under the nearest desk. Under a desk felt like my natural habitat anyway, among all the cables and plug sockets and the gentle hum of computer towers. Amy watched through thickly mascaraed fake eyelashes as I looked the machine over.

There was a dent on one side, very much high heel shaped. I checked Amy's shoes.

'Did you, um, happen to kick this printer?'

'You have to kick it,' she explained very patiently as if it were she and not me who worked on the tech support desk. 'That's how you get the headed paper out.'

'I don't think kicking was in the manual.'

Amy smiled very fakely. 'You're funny. Can you just fix it?'

I damn well tried. I unplugged it. I replugged it. I reset the spooler. I changed the toner. I reinstalled the print drivers.

The printer stayed dead. Amy became annoyed because

she would now have to walk downstairs to collect her recipe printout.

'Why can't you just buy an iPrinter?' she asked, exasperated and thinking of her beloved iPhone I had gradually made idiot-proof.

I wanted to say something like "I hope your poor little legs don't get tired walking downstairs to collect your non-work related printing" but I never say what I want to irate colleagues.

Instead I said, 'No one in the office uses Macs for work, so it wouldn't be compatible.'

She was already gone, being one of those people who doesn't stick around to see what the other person replies.

I looked at the printer. *ERR*, said the little screen on the front.

'Hi Josie,' said Nick. His laptop bag was slung over his shoulder and he had his coat on. He probably had an important client meeting. I liked Nick. Firstly because he hired me. And secondly because he knew how to use Google. 'That's a damning expression. Are you alright?'

'I think this printer's had it.'

Nick looked at the printer, a square, off-white beast of a machine. I felt like it was looking back, defiant. *ERR*.

'Have you been down to the Basement?'

Dread creeped over my skin. 'No. Not yet.'

Nick raised his eyebrows.

'I will. If I have to.'

When no one was looking, I kicked the printer. It deserved it for making me look stupid in front of Amy and Nick.

***

I put off doing anything with the printer for as long as I could. But Nick caught me again soon enough.

'Reckon you can get the printer going for us today? Amy really needs to print her recipes out,' said Nick. 'It's business critical. Right after Sandra prints off every single email she got last week.'

'It's almost like they *want* to destroy the planet.'

'It's in our company mission statement. An ambitious, innovative and collaborative goal, don't you think?'

I managed a smile. More people should have bosses with a sense of humour.

To my delight, my laptop picked up the printer straight away. After some fiddling, the printer made happy whirring noises (as opposed to "I'm going to break" whirring noises). I printed a test sheet. It came out perfect.

For one beautiful moment, I thought everything was going to be alright.

And then the tickets started.

***

(46 unread tickets)

Cant print. SOS.

Spreadsheets printing search history?

Printer status reads 'cba'

Printer is a joke!

URGENT FIX PRINTER BY 9:30AM (sent from iPhone at 9:28AM)

Printout of lyrics to Humans Are Dead?

***

Honestly, I had no clue where to start. Maybe the printer wasn't connected to our network and we were receiving the printing of some other office? One with some right weirdos, judging by the tickets.

I opened Command Prompt and typed a ping command. This was how we checked if machines were connected. The prompt was supposed to either list a bunch of technical information or throw up an error.

The black screen typed, slowly, letter by letter:

your mothers so stupid
she went to the dentist
to get Bluetooth

My mother had a degree in law and knew all the answers on Pointless. I did not take the insult to heart. I checked the firewalls and ran the antivirus software. Nothing came up. We hadn't been hacked.

I typed the ping command again. Maybe I'd imagined the response. The printer tickets were tiring me out. It was possible I was going mad.

your mothers so stupid
she put airbags on her computer
in case it crashed

Actually, I could see some of my colleagues trying that. Then I stopped laughing because this was quite frankly pretty strange and I had another 23 tickets about the printer.

I opened Google and typed "printer telling me your mother jokes".

It gave me printable lists of jokes. Not very helpful to anyone over the age of eleven. Maybe we'd been invisibly hacked by an eleven year-old?

I thought about the Basement. But I wanted to make sure I'd exhausted all my other options first.

When I tried reinstalling the printer drivers, I got an error box with a red X simply saying "Fuck off". Well. How rude.

I opened Google and typed "printer error fuck off".

Nothing useful. No forum replies and of course no Microsoft help pages. I decided to take one last look at the printer for signs of physical tampering. I didn't know what else to do.

***

Mayhem had broken out by the printer. Five of my colleagues stood clutching bits of paper and talking in cross voices. When they saw me, they fell silent. All of them looked like they wanted to kill me.

'This is disgusting! It's not my quarterly report at all!' shrieked one of the bosses who was not as cool as Nick.

I took the page from her. It was a list of PornHub searches. I raised an eyebrow. Her cheeks flushed bright red.

'It's the printer! There's something wrong with it!'

She had me there. The printer definitely wasn't functioning normally.

'I need my recipe but all it will print is one for gluten free fish fingers and custard!' Amy said crossly.

I sent them all away, saying I needed some time to examine the wayward machine. I poked about, checking the trays and fiddling with the buttons on the display.

'Please, please can you just print the stuff in the queue,' I begged. 'I have 116 tickets! 116!'

The printer did nothing. I did not sense any sympathy.

'God! What do you want from me?' I yelled at the printer.

It whirred. Clicked. A sheet of paper emerged.

SURRENDER, it said.

I blinked. Read it again.

'Like hell I will!'

I pulled the power plug from its socket. The mechanical hum died and for a moment I felt smug, as if I'd won. As if the torment wouldn't begin all over again as soon as I switched it back on.

Unless...maybe it was too much to hope but sometimes the techie's ultimate creed came through for us. Could turning it off and on again save me?

I plugged the printer back in. I held my breath as the display came on. It whirred. Another piece of paper came out.

SURRENDER

'Fuck!'

"Printer told me to surrender", I typed into Google. The results once again were useless. If only it needed toner or paper or drivers or anything normal!

A clack of heels.

'Why are you yelling? Did you get my lasagna recipe?' asked Amy. 'I really need it, my mother-in-law is coming to dinner.'

'No! Go downstairs!'

'Alright! God, no need to shout at me, it's not my fault!'

I knew what I needed to do. I had no choice.

I needed to go to the Basement.

***

I took my special swipe card and blew off a layer of dust. I put on my coat and changed my Teams status to "Away". I ignored the receptionists who in turn ignored me as I held my card up to the sensor on the door that led into the guts of our office building. Somehow the usually positive bleep seemed menacing.

I walked down the steps. The air became cold and stale. I wanted to turn back to the bright office lights and breezy aircon. But I pushed on until I came to the main room, dark apart from the glare of LEDs upon the server banks.

A swivel chair creaked. A haggard face turned in my direction.

'Is that you Rebecca?' Steve, head of IT, creaked out.

'No, it's Josie. Rebecca left years ago.'

Steve's face dropped. He'd been working in this basement thirty years and I had it on good authority Rebecca's was the only name he remembered. Some said she was the love of his life, tragically tempted away for a promotion in the Big Smoke. Others said she was fired after looting microchips to sell on eBay.

'Jodie. What can I do for you?'

Computers in various states of disassembly covered the desk. A digital graveyard.

'It's a printer issue.'

I handed him the piece of paper with the word *SURRENDER* printed on it.

'Google's got nothing,' I told him. He cackled. I'd never heard him make that noise before. I had my hand in my pocket ready to dial 999 before I realised he was laughing and not having a heart attack.

'What do you think, Jodie? Do we surrender?'

'No?' I suggested helplessly.

'No,' he agreed. 'I'm going to need some special tools for this.'

Steve turned out a crate of wires and fished through them

until he came up with something that looked like a fishing hook attached to an ethernet cable.

'Know what this is?'

I shook my head.

'Bring me the printer.'

'It's too big.'

Steve let out a long hiss through his teeth. 'Fine. I suppose it has been a few years since I walked among our colleagues. Maybe they'll have forgotten who I am by now.'

***

Walking through the office with Steve was like trailing after a celebrity. Quite frankly it was weirding me out almost as much as the sweary printer.

'Steve! My man! I don't suppose you could take a look at my monitor—'

'Hey Steve, can you get me a new phone, this one's out of storage?'

'Steve! Steve! I need you to install Spotify. I've got a business case ready to go.'

Steve brushed them off with a hello and a request to submit a ticket. I felt rather sore thinking of my queue going up yet again.

After what felt like aeons, we made it to the printer. Steve unplugged it.

'I already tried that,' I said and he grunted.

The strange hooked cable glowed a luminous LED green.

'Bastards,' he said. 'Shouldn't have come back here.'

He tossed the hook at the printer and I winced, waiting for the smack of plastic on plastic. It never came. Instead the hook disappeared inside the body of the printer. I was pretty sure physics had broken somehow.

'You're lucky,' Steve said gruffly. 'Do you know what they did to Rebecca?'

'Huh? Who did what?'

'The infestation was crippling. They got into every keyboard, every monitor. I tried to save her, but I was too late.'

'Save her?'

All I could think of was the floppy disk icon. I thought of the overflowing box of floppies in Steve's office and wondered if Rebecca was somehow *saved* on one of them. A chilling thought.

There was a hard tug on the cable. Steve's wrinkled face slashed into a smile. He reeled in the cable with a brisk flick of his wrist.

The hook exploded out of the printer. Attached to the end was a wriggling creature, a tiny man shape wearing a hat with horns. The hook went through the back of his strange crimson coat.

'Your mother's so stupid she went to the beach to surf the internet!' he squeaked in tiny chipmunk tones. Then he spat a tiny bubble which landed on my shoe.

Steve sighed. 'You got friends in there, young'un?'

The tiny man folded his arms. 'I don't need 'em. I like living on my own.'

'Well, you can't live here. I have a service level agreement signed by the Gremlin King after the Cyber War of 2002.'

'Lies! This place will be mine!'

'I won the war,' said Steve. 'And I'll win again if you try and infest my turf.'

The gremlin squinted his eyebrows. 'What can a human do?'

Steve stamped his foot. The gremlin's eyes got very big.

'It's you! Steve the Stamper! Monster! Murderer!'

'I'll never forget how I found my Rebecca all those years ago, weeping in the stationery cupboard. She was a broken woman. Days of misprints, broken monitors, malfunctioning keyboards and rude emails drove her to madness. Nothing could bring her back to me. She was the best assistant I ever had! You got what you deserved!'

Steve shot a glance at me, at my agape mouth. 'No offence. You're not a terrible assistant or anything.'

I wasn't technically his assistant, but whatever. An argument for another day.

'You're not really going to stamp on him are you?'

The gremlin squirmed on the hook in utter, desperate terror.

Steve shook his head. 'Nah. He's just a young'un. I've got a plan in mind.'

***

'Sorry Josie, can't stop!' Nick gave me an apologetic wave. 'I'll sign that all off later.'

I nodded and placed the stack of new equipment forms on his overflowing desk.

'Business is crazy. Our nearest competitor has been plagued with never-ending IT issues so they're out of the game. It's a good job we've got you and Steve to keep us going.'

'You're welcome.'

On Nick's desk, I caught a glimpse of a document titled "Salary review". Steve and I were listed at the top and the numbers were looking good. Nick was a great boss. Though maybe not so great at GDPR compliance.

Also, I really had to hand it to Steve. He'd masterfully engineered a situation where everybody left happy. I hoped the gremlin liked his new home, though I had to admit it seemed ethically dubious.

'What if someone else ends up like Rebecca?' I asked Steve.

'Rebecca married a loser, I mean lawyer, and is doing very well in her marketing career. Some folk simply aren't meant to fight gremlins.'

'I can fight them,' I promised. 'Teach me everything you know. But first, I need to help Amy print a recipe.'

The Owners of the Tree

Twelve minutes discussing the colour of wheelie bins, and all the while Derek's cheap plastic chair left painful marks on his thighs. Why did they have to hold parish council meetings in the school hall? He could almost hear the clatter of footsteps and shriek of teenage hysteria as five hundred children thundered between classrooms and bullied each other to conform to an ever-changing standard. For those with thick glasses, a stutter and a tendency to remain plump, that standard could never be reached. At least NHS monstrosity frames were a thing of the past. Derek had new glasses now, rectangular with thin silver frames. The optician called them stylish. He wasn't sure he'd go that far.

The chair of the council produced a sack from beneath the table. It looked like Father Christmas's bag of presents. She tucked a curl of greying hair behind her ear and then announced with great solemnity, 'As you all know, we have invited a special guest to the meeting. Please welcome Derek from the Association of Fey Relations.'

A polite and unnecessary round of applause. Derek smiled and nodded and wished everyone would stop looking at him and go back to their biscuits.

'These are all the complaints about the tree,' said the chair. She presented him with the sack. 'And this is without Facebook posts, emails and complaints to our community radio station.'

Everyone on the council started talking at once.

'Blasted tree.'

'Why is it not gone?'

'What's the problem this time?'

The chair hushed them, as though they were noisy children. Perhaps she was a teacher. She looked like a teacher. 'The latest bulldozer met an unfortunate end when some youths drove it into the cashpoint at the newsagents.'

The tree in question had a trunk so thick it would take five, maybe six people to join hands and hug it. It had the drooping branches of a willow and tiny star-shaped leaves like a sycamore. It provided shelter from rain and shade in the sun. The air nearby stood crisp and still. Birds did not nest in it, cats did not climb it. All sound apart from the rustling of leaves ceased when one stood in its shadow. It dropped big branches on any car who dared park under it and threatened the foundations of nearby buildings with its roots. Children who tried to climb it soon found themselves falling, and teens who wanted to carve their initials on its trunk accidentally carved up their own hands instead.

A few months ago, when the complaint first found its way to his inbox, Derek had suggested putting up a safety perimeter. A cordon of plastic garden string and an overly wordy sign had warned people away from tree-based disaster. But now the tree and its perimeter occupied a rather large space bang-smack in the middle of the village. People complained about how annoying it was to walk/drive/bike around and why couldn't the space be put to better use? Then came the people from Tesco. They looked very serious and did a lot of nodding and measuring things. They told the council how much money they would pay for the land. *Without* the tree on it.

The council had been trying to get rid of the tree for months. Meanwhile, two bulldozers ended up in ditches, three suddenly had flat tyres and now this one had crashed into the newsagents. Not to mention all the tree-surgeons who'd gone missing after their sat-navs went awry, or all the working chainsaws that mysteriously broke down within a metre of the trunk...

'And you're quite sure it was youths who hijacked the bulldozer?'

'Who else could it have been, Derek?' asked Marlene Sutton. She'd been the year above him at school, a pretty girl with her pick of boyfriends. Age had creased her terribly. He wondered if she thought the same about him. 'You're not telling me your piddly little fairy friends can drive a bulldozer? There's a lot at stake here.'

'And we want to buy a new coffee machine,' said the chair. 'For everyone. Not just for council meetings,' she added hastily.

'If you can "see fairies" or whatever,' said Marlene, rolling her eyes, 'you need to get them to understand our position.'

Again, the school hall surroundings made him uncomfortable. A girl who could see fairies was one thing. A boy was quite another. Hopefully Marlene wouldn't stuff his satchel down the toilet.

'What do *you* suggest we do, Derek?' said the chair, very gently. She always lowered her voice to talk to him, as though he might bolt. 'If we don't get rid of the tree, Tesco will pull out of the deal. At this point, I'm willing to try anything. Will you talk to...*them*...for us?'

'That's my job,' he said as smoothly as he could. 'As I've been *gifted* with the sight, I'm in a unique position to negotiate.'

'What a load of old cobblers,' muttered Marlene. 'Not much point him talking to himself, is there?'

The chair smiled very kindly as they all ignored Marlene. 'I heard you grew up here. Is it good to be back?'

No, he thought. History pulled at him around every corner. The patch of stinging nettles where he'd fallen off his bike. The climbing frame he'd been too afraid to reach the top of. The house he used to live in, where the door was painted a different colour and the once neatly kept garden had lost the battle against a tangle of weeds.

It didn't feel good at all.

'Yes, lovely,' he said.

***

'I know you're here,' Derek said to the chilly air, when really he knew no such thing.

He let out an indignant huff. He pulled a notebook and pen from his satchel and began to scribble a note addressed: *To the owner of this tree.*

His handwriting looked like a tangle of spiders. Perhaps he'd better get the notice printed. He fixed it to the trunk with a flap of sticky tape and hoped the fairies who lived nearby could read.

It had been a long time since he'd been up close to the tree like this. He moved the densest branches aside and sat on a familiar hollow in the grass, setting the tray of acorns beside him. A thousand ghosts of past-Dereks made him shiver. His tormentors never found him here.

A puff of air steamed up his glasses. He frowned. Took them off, wiped them over. As he was about to put them back on, they tumbled from his hands. He fumbled in the grass but they leapt from his grip. A faint giggle accompanied the rustle of leaves. Someone was clearly enjoying his Velma-from-*Scooby-Doo* routine.

'Is someone there?' he said. 'You're not funny, you know. I've played this game a hundred times before.'

'I thought we weren't talking,' said a tiny, musical voice. 'Being ignored is also a classic bullying tactic so it's tit for tat, yes?'

A tiny, blurred ball of light danced before his eyes. He finally reached his glasses and the world shifted back into focus. The fairy was about six inches tall, dressed in a gown of leaves and pink geraniums. Her fair hair was tied into a cluster of plaits and she wore a minute scowl. Her wings were pearlescent where the light hit them and beat fast enough to emit a faint buzz. It had been years, but he knew her immediately.

'I wasn't ignoring you,' Derek managed. 'I was *avoiding* you. You always got me in trouble at school.'

'You didn't like the butterflies in your lunchbox? The embroidery on your sports kit?'

The little fairy looked so genuinely hurt Derek couldn't help but feel sorry for her.

'Well, not really. It all made life very difficult. But I would like to make amends.'

He offered her a spice filled acorn from the bag he'd brought with him.

'Ah. You pick your gifts well. I am called Acorn. Now we are speaking, I can properly introduce myself.' Her eyes narrowed. 'You want something.'

'I'm a representative employed by the parish council,' said Derek. 'I've come about the tree.'

Acorn puffed out her cheeks. 'The tree is under fey protection.'

'The council would like you to reconsider. They believe a supermarket would be of great benefit to the village. Also they really want a new coffee machine for council meetings. Er, I mean everyone.'

'What do *you* think?'

To his surprise, he answered honestly. 'I like the tree. It always protected me.'

She smiled. 'I like it too. I am sure the King will be in agreement. I suppose you would like something official stating as much?'

'I think that would be best.'

She completed a series of complex looking air acrobatics. The outline of a door appeared in the tree trunk. Derek tentatively touched the handle. It felt warm, like it had been left out in the sun. He pushed down the handle, took a deep breath and put his foot over the threshold. The acorn tray wobbled in his other hand.

***

The air felt very dense and smelt strongly of pollen. Derek

sneezed and reached for the handkerchief stuffed up his sleeve. They were in a corridor with white walls and a long line of paintings. Above he could see a clear, blue sky instead of a ceiling.

'This is inside the tree?'

'The tree marks the portal to the Fairy-King's palace. Wait here.'

The paintings showed a series of watercolour portraits of fairies in feathered crowns. They were surrounded by butter-flies, wildflower meadows, autumn leaves... Before he made it to the end of the paintings, Acorn flitted back in front of him.

'In accordance with the Fey-Human treaty, His Majesty grants you an audience. This way, please.'

Derek expected something with marble statues and vast paintings. Like Buckingham Palace crossed with the Parthe-non. Instead he walked through a glass door into a gleam-ing wood-panelled room. A vast screen bigger than Derek's kitchen sat at one end, flashing through a series of adverts for television programmes. The rest of the room was decorated with posters displaying the chiselled faces of famous actors. A popcorn machine crackled merrily away in the background.

'Bow before the Fairy-King,' hissed Acorn.

Derek hadn't seen him at first. But there he was, reclining in a mini leather chair on a glass-topped coffee table. Instead of more traditional garb like Acorn, he was decked out in a biker jacket with wing holes cut in the back, jeans and tiny Converse shoes.

Derek bowed and set down his bag of acorns.

'I present to you the human named Derek, of the Briwood line,' said Acorn.

'Sweet! Derek. My man. My dude. You're the first human in this village to ask for an audience in about a hundred years. Way to go!'

The Fairy-King presented a tiny fist. Derek frowned. Acorn fluttered up in front of him and demonstrated what the kids called a "fist bump" or "brofist". Derek carefully completed the manoeuvre, trying very hard not to punch the King clean out of his chair.

'So tell me, my man. What is it I can do for you?'

Derek wet his lips. 'The village want to cut down the tree so they can sell the land and build a Tesco.'

The King harrumphed. 'Begone, gutless knave! I hath cleansed my blade once this day and I do not wish to do so again.'

Acorn cleared her throat. 'Your Majesty, according to the treaty all threats must be submitted in writing.'

'Oh, right. Let me put it another way. The tree is ours,' said His Majesty. 'We are going to need something seriously spectacular in order to even think about replacing it. You get me?'

'...Not at all. I mean, I can discuss giving you a share of the money but—'

'I careth not for your mortal money!' The Fairy-King spat. 'What I wish for—no, what I demand—is something much better.'

'To tell the truth, I thought you might continue to protect the tree. It's an important part of the village's history. I think the village is lovely the way it is.'

The Fairy-King shrugged. 'It's just a tree, dude. Right, Acorn?'

She hesitated. 'If I might speak frankly, Your Majesty?' He nodded. 'This tree was planted by your great-grandmother, the first fairy queen of the village. It's provided us with shelter, comfort and food for many a year. It would be a great loss for us. Not something to be taken lightly.'

'I know not why people are so shy about moving forwards these days,' muttered the Fairy-King. 'Come on guys, embrace the future! No point living in the past, is there?'

***

Derek stumbled out of the palace, through the portal and back into the real world with a sinking sense of disappointment. He'd done his job by getting permission from the Fairy-King to remove the tree. He wished he hadn't. He should never have taken this job, never have come back to this village.

'So that's it. The tree's going to die,' said Acorn. Her voice cracked.

'No,' said Derek, his voice dark. 'I was always scared to stand up for myself in this place. But the tree stood up for me, gave me a safe hiding place over and over again. I have to save it. It's only right.'

***

An emergency parish council meeting was called.

'The main item on the agenda is the tree, of course,' said the chair. 'Over to Derek from the Association of Fey Relations.'

'Good afternoon, ladies and gents. Accompanying me today is Acorn, though of course you cannot see her.'

The chair smiled politely as always. Marlene looked bored. The other council members were munching on chocolate digestive biscuits or sipping their teas.

'Acorn is here to relay a message from the Fairy-King, which I will recite to you.'

Derek shot Acorn a glance. She nodded. They were ready.

'Hello, humans. Please do bog off and leave our tree be. It is a protective force for fey and humans alike. We do not go around knocking your houses down. Usually. Failure to comply will result in an unusual curse—'

Acorn snapped her fingers. The council members began coughing and spluttering.

'—as I have just demonstrated. Any foodstuffs you ingest will turn into nothing but ground cinnamon.'

Derek turned to the pitcher of water he'd fetched beforehand and began pouring out glasses. No one seemed particularly grateful.

'Where is the little bugger?' growled Marlene. 'I've had it up to here with fairies. Show yourself, coward!'

'Fairies only show themselves to those who are worth talking to,' snapped Acorn. Derek decided not to relay it. They were likely in enough trouble. The chair was the only one who did not look angry, only disappointed.

For a moment, Derek wondered if they'd done the right thing.

'Hang on,' said the bloke typing the meeting minutes. His fingers were frozen over the keys of his laptop. 'I've just received an email into the council inbox. It's from the Fairy-King.'

***

Derek watched the great yellow "M" sign being hoisted by workmen into the space the great tree once stood. A few star shaped leaves remained trodden into the ground. Every other trace of the tree had been removed. It had taken only three days.

'T'is a shame,' said Acorn, fluttering at his shoulder. He felt her sad sigh against his cheek. 'I really thought your plan might work.'

The centre of the village had turned from a quiet, hushed place into a hubbub of activity. The scent of fresh chicken nuggets drifted on the breeze. Delighted teens pelted each other with french fries. Older folk peered dubiously down at their cardboard cups of tea.

A woman in uniform stormed out of the glass doors. 'Alright, who put sugar on the fries this time? And can you please stop messing with the ketchup tap, it looks like a crime scene in there!'

Derek heard the faint sound of tinkling fairy laughter. Acorn rolled her eyes.

'I never would have guessed the Fairy-King had such a taste for fast food,' sighed Derek.

'I should have realised His Highness will do anything for a Big Mac. His new-fangled ways sent his poor mother to an early grave.'

'Oh, well. I suppose everybody wins. The parish council have their coffee machine money and the fairy folk have 24-hour fast food. What a world we live in!'

Acorn made a "hmm" of agreement. Her face looked rainier than Devon in November. He knew the feeling.

'I'm sorry I ignored you for all those years,' he said. 'I just thought it would be easier. I was a coward.'

'...If anyone bullies you again, I'll put spiders in their shoes.'

'Thanks.' They stood in brief, contemplative silence. 'I'll treat you,' Derek said, reaching for his wallet. 'What do you fancy?'

'Well,' said Acorn, looking sheepish. 'I have been wondering what a 'McFlurry' is...'

The Sound of Breaking

Juliet remembered Beth saying "The true test for a relationship is putting a tent up together". Buzzing conversation from surrounding campers provided a stark contrast to their near-silent campsite. Mud, sweat, collapsing tents and endless cans of stale beer clinking into the night awaited them. Juliet had met Beth at this festival and they'd attended every year since. This was their beginning. Juliet didn't want them to end. She wasn't ready. She'd never be ready.

When the last tent peg was done, Juliet leaned in for a kiss but Beth turned her head away. That was when Juliet knew it really was over between them. She tried to keep it together even as her words came out in a violent splurge.

'You know how much I love you. And you won't even kiss me!'

Beth's hair stuck up where she hadn't slept properly, like she'd been zapped with electricity.

'So we're finally doing this.'

Juliet's mind stuttered but it kept looping round to one dreadful truth, one image of Beth turning away from her.

'You won't even kiss me!'

'We can't keep pretending we're the same people we used

to be. There's so much I want to do…and you don't. You just keep dreaming, Juliet.'

'And what's wrong with that?'

'I want someone who isn't standing still. You always say you want to be a singer, but you won't do an open mic night, you won't audition for bands. You wouldn't set foot in the recording studio when I paid for a session.'

'You should have asked! I wasn't ready!'

'You're never going to be ready, because it's never going to be easy. The only reason you're still with me is because no one better has come along yet.'

'You don't mean that.'

'This whole trip we've been going back to our old hang-outs and talking about the past. If we were really going to stay together, we'd have been talking about the future.'

Anything Juliet wanted to say faded into nothing. The wave of despair she'd been holding back for days, weeks, months crashed over her. Why wasn't she crying? She should be crying.

'You'll be alright,' said Beth. 'There's no point dragging this out anymore than we already have. I'm going home.'

*＊＊

Beth left most of the camping stuff. Juliet had no idea how to use most of it without her. She did know how to unzip the sleeping bag and crawl inside.

Her mind played an unhelpful reel of moments from her relationship, as if she'd just been voted off a reality show. She could almost hear a smarmy presenter saying "Here are your highlights."

Beth asking her to dance, Beth gazing at her as she sang in

the car where no one else could hear. Beth wrestling with the giant sleeping bag, too big for one person.

The world was made for couples. Everything from working in pairs at school to renting a property as an adult. How was she supposed to do anything on her own? Even this trip, which had been her idea, required Beth's help. Juliet couldn't drive. She'd always had someone to ferry her from one place to the other, first her mother and then Beth. What was she supposed to do now?

She got out her phone and looked through her contacts. She paused over *Mum*. She imagined herself curled up on her mum's sofa sobbing the story out over hot chocolate. It made it seem too real when surely it must all be a nightmare. Any minute she'd wake up, any minute now.

***

When, after yet another night of separate activities in separate rooms, she'd suggested to Beth that they go for an extended holiday, she hadn't meant for it to turn out like this.

'Would that make you happy?' Beth asked. Juliet promised it would.

It hadn't worked. Juliet tried so hard not to argue that she went along with everything Beth suggested, from breakfast to the music on her ancient car's CD player. They got stuck in Exeter's one-way system and Beth remarked on how her life was stuck in a one-way system, going around and around but never forward. Juliet nodded and pretended she understood. Then they walked too far too fast and Juliet's sandals cut bloody lines into her feet.

'Where's your voice, Juliet?' Beth complained as she

furiously applied Savlon. 'Why don't you ever tell me these things?'

'You wanted to see the Mermaid Chair.'

'You've always been like this. Going along with whatever is easiest. Sometimes I feel like I barely know you.'

Juliet stayed silent. Then she said, 'Remember when we walked along the beach in the snow and I wasn't wearing waterproof shoes so my feet went blue.'

Beth patted her knee, which Juliet took to mean she was impatient but fond. They looked at the mermaid carved into shiny wood, the chair they'd come so far to see. The plaque said she'd taken the boy with the most beautiful voice in the church to live with her in the sea. Juliet wondered what she'd found so exceptional about Beth. She couldn't remember.

***

Juliet ignored the kaleidoscope of Beths running through her mind and sent a text message. To Beth, of course, because there was no one else she wanted to talk to.

I want things to be like they were before.

I want something new. We don't make each other happy.

Juliet hadn't expected a reply. She thought Beth would be driving. She looked at the words on the screen for several long minutes and realised she couldn't argue against them. She couldn't even remember what *happy* was like.

'Oi, oi! Anyone here?' yelled a voice from outside. 'Wouldn't happen to have a corkscrew, would ya mate?'

There was a corkscrew in the camping bag. No one could accuse Beth of being ill-prepared. Juliet dug it out and crawled to the tent flaps.

A guy waited outside, wearing a Hawaiian shirt so bright it hurt Juliet's eyes, paired with chinos and battered trainers.

'The music's starting soon, are you coming?' he asked. 'Have a drink on us if you want, my girlfriend bought some decent wine.'

Juliet glanced back at the dark hole of her tent, where she could lie and reminisce and maybe cry in peace. Then she looked into the bright sunshine, the bright tents and the bright people whose spirits hadn't yet become muddy and impatient.

'OK,' she said, even though she ached at the word "girl-friend".

She thought maybe she finally understood what people meant when they said "I need a freakin' drink."

***

The wine left Juliet with a pleasant warm buzz. She flashed back and forth between sinking and floating. One moment she cared about Beth and the next she didn't. It was confusing, but better. The world no longer felt like it would crush her.

Her new companions wanted to go to the main stage but the crash of guitars made her think too much of Beth. She meandered by herself.

At the festival's edge, Juliet found a stage set up with a karaoke machine. *Heartbreak Hotel,* read the banner. Juliet always hated *I Will Survive* but she lingered as a woman her mother's age belted out the words in a long tuneless warble. For all her longing to be a singer, she'd never stepped on a stage. Beth was right, it was stupid. She should do it. She *could* do it. Right now. And that would prove that she was going somewhere, moving forward. Then maybe Beth would come back. Say she'd been wrong. Say she wanted to carry on with their life together.

A clamour of hands went up for a turn with the microphone once *I Will Survive* ended, but the honours went to a stunning woman dressed in pastels. Her forget-me-not blue skirt billowed so much she looked as though she might float away. Her hair shone gold in the artificial light. Juliet stepped closer.

The song was slow, seductive, the music seeping into Juliet like warm honey. The lyrics were something about the world having teeth and life being caught in its jaws. But it wasn't about the words, it was the woman's velvet voice that made the song magical. Juliet felt like she'd heard it before, a long time ago, but she wasn't sure where or when.

The singer caught her eye. And smiled. Held the microphone out for her.

This was her chance.

'Will you record me?' she asked, holding out her phone. The woman nodded.

'I can tell you're going to be good.'

Juliet couldn't place her accent, but it didn't matter. With shaking hands, she took the stage, microphone clenched in her fist.

***

Juliet looked down at the crowd. Some of the crowd looked back. The rest looked at phones or drinks or shouted at their friends. Even though Juliet was the one on stage, she felt small and unimportant. The woman holding her phone smiled, gave her an encouraging nod.

Juliet searched for her voice.

'I just broke up with my girlfriend,' she said, then winced as her words boomed through the microphone.

Some of the crowd raised their bottles and cans.

'Men suck!' yelled a woman with silvery bracelets.

'So do women!' yelled a long-haired biker dude.

Juliet swallowed. The music started. She sang. Her voice quivered but the crowd was patient with her. She sang a funeral song with the wrong words, but to her it felt apt. A breakup wasn't as final as death, but the grief that followed carried echoes of such a loss.

At the song's end, tears slipped down her cheeks. The cheering crowd blurred. Someone took the microphone from her but she couldn't seem to move.

The woman with the honey-song helped her down from the stage. She smelt fresh like sea salt and somehow Juliet remembered to breathe.

***

'Let's get you a drink,' said the woman, handing back her phone. 'You were perfect, just perfect. What's your name?'

Juliet managed to sniffle it out. The woman introduced herself as Morveren and procured Juliet a plastic cup of beer that tasted like peanut butter. It was foul and Juliet shuddered at every sip as Morveren watched with sympathetic eyes.

'I loved her so much,' Juliet said. And then, 'You're gorgeous, who broke up with you?'

'A boy I met every week in church. He sang so beautifully, you see. I asked him to run away with me, but he got on a ship to America instead.'

'He sounds dumb.'

'I still love him. Just like you and your white rose.'

Juliet thumbed at her phone and hit *send* to Beth on the video of her karaoke performance.

I sang in front of people. Is that what you wanted?

The message changed to *read* straight away but no little typing icon came up. Juliet made a feral noise of annoyance. She dropped her phone into her beer and watched the screen flash a couple of times before dimming into darkness.

'Oh, sweetheart,' said Morveren. 'You might need that, don't you think?'

'No,' said Juliet. 'I'm done. Fuck her! She never put the dishes in the right cupboard and she stopped being pretty three years ago when she dyed her hair black.'

This realisation made her sob. Morveren patted her shoulder.

'Come with me,' she said and Juliet nodded. What else was she going to do?

***

Juliet followed Morveren away from the crowds and down a narrow path between two cliffs. She should have felt frightened, perhaps, with the festival crowd only a distant hum in the background and the sky scarlet with the setting sun. The whistling wind lifted her hair and cut right through her jacket, made for style and not warmth. Any moment she'd surely wake to the stink and sirens of London with Beth beside her, warm in bed.

DANGER
UNSTABLE CLIFFS.

Juliet hesitated.

'Almost there,' said Morveren as she started picking her way down. 'Step where I step.'

'I don't want to fall.'

'I won't let you.'

The honey was back in her voice. Juliet followed.

They came out into a small bay. The sand was pale and unmarked. The only sounds were of the surf and the seagulls. Morveren walked out into the waves without a care for her skirt. The garment stuck to her legs as the water weighed it down.

'Come on,' Morveren said again and Juliet followed. Her jeans grew heavy as she let the water rise to her waist. It felt pleasantly cool, like balm for her wounded soul.

'Sing for me,' said Morveren. 'Anything.'

Juliet sniffled, laughed and picked the latest lovelorn, regret-filled anthem. Morveren added her voice to the chorus as the sea sighed around them.

'As I thought. Nothing tempers a voice like a broken heart. There's a reason all the greatest songs in the world are about tragic romances and lost lovers.'

Juliet shivered. She'd heard that before, hadn't she? Beth had once asked Juliet if she wanted to sing about sex or sadness with the wicked laugh she didn't use anymore. They had both changed.

Morveren smiled. 'Look at me.'

She swam around Juliet in a circle. The skirt was gone and that was...a tail streaming behind her. Juliet blinked. Shook her head. Her mind flashed back to the church in Zennor. The carving on the chair. Half woman, half fish. But it couldn't be true.

'You're playing a trick on me,' she whispered.

'Your singing will make the sea sound so much sweeter.'

Morveren surged to a stop and kissed her, with passion. Juliet had forgotten kissing when it was new, all teeth and tongue, noses and chins banging together because they hadn't learned each other's rhythm. Morveren tasted like salt and Juliet wanted to keep tasting it, forever. Her mouth felt like it was moving of its own accord as she savoured every drop of moisture on Morveren's lips.

'I followed your voice all along the Cornish coast, every day a little sadder. You're just what I've been looking for.'

Juliet closed her eyes. Yes. The sea called to her, it wanted her voice. Morveren's warm hand held hers, her lips ghosted against Juliet's forehead. They wanted her voice so badly. She just needed to let it out.

'Alright. I'll sing for you. For a little while.'

But there were so many songs about broken hearts that she stayed until dawn and still there were more. And more after the next dawn too. And the next. And finally, finally, after the festival was done and her throat was raw, Morveren touched Juliet's cheek and said, 'You're one of us now. Let me take you home.'

Juliet looked out to sea and saw how full of broken hearts it was. Broken hearts happened every minute of every hour of every week, so she was far from alone. The thought buoyed her. With a swish of her new tail, she swam away.

The Curse of the Unicorn

April 2020, 1 month after COVID-19 lockdown

The picture on the computer screen made Kel's breath catch. The glowing lights of London against an impossible creature. She examined it from every angle, looking for tell-tale signs of Photoshop. But there were no seams, no strange fuzzy corners. There were multiple pictures, multiple angles, multiple timestamps. It was everything she had hoped for.

Hunter: I saw it again last night. Isn't it beautiful?

MsSparkles: I can't believe how irresponsible you are, going out at a time like this.

Hunter: Don't you get it? A time like this is the only time I'll get my chance. I can't exactly go trekking off into the forest whenever I fancy.

TitaniaJr: I guess the quiet of the lockdown must have drawn it into the city. Do you think it's lonely?

Kel had seen all she needed. She slammed the laptop shut. The long empty days of being furloughed meant she'd been free to scour the web for hours and at last her efforts had paid off. Thanks to this motley collection of strangers on a long-forgotten forum, she knew exactly where and when she'd find what she was looking for.

Kel took one last look at the place she'd called home for the last few miserable years. The hot water took ages to work, the windows wouldn't open, it was freezing in winter. She'd had too many nightmares where every time she went out the front door she only ended up at the bottom of the stairs, climbing back up to the shabby flat with no way to escape.

She hoisted her backpack which contained all she needed; a few clothes, a wallet, a phone to help her navigate. Her car was loaded with a sleeping bag, blankets, a torch and spare batteries.

On the way out, Kel held her sleek silver laptop over the stair rail. She gave it one last hateful stare. Then it tumbled three stories before cracking on the threadbare carpet.

No more Teams. No more Zoom. No more artificially bedraggled politicians chatting shit while being unable to work their own slideshow presentations.

Old Mrs Hubbard banged out of her ground floor flat, walking stick whapping the ground. 'What's going on now?'

'Just an accident,' Kel explained as she came down the stairs.

The woman's beady eyes roved over Kel. 'You can't go out, it's not safe. And it's the law. There are police, you know, on the main road out of town. My son told me.'

'I won't take the main road then.'

Mrs Hubbard folded her arms. 'You could at least take your rubbish with you.'

Kel swept out, giving the remains of the machine an extra spiteful stamp. Years of Mrs Hubbard nagging Kel about where she parked her car and how loudly she climbed the stairs made it incredibly satisfying to see her lost for words.

Ever since lockdown Kel's road had been eerily quiet. Cars lined either side of the road like stones in a graveyard.

Kel located her battered Honda Jazz. Dirt cheap to run and drive, they'd been through a lot together. Three years of driving through uni, three years of thankless commute to a bland office block in a blander retail park through gridlocked traffic and the car still purred when Kel started it, like it was pleased to see her.

Curtains twitched as people looked out at the sound of her car engine. Kel took a deep breath and pulled out of parallel park none too carefully. The car in front sported a new scrape. Kel didn't bother with a note.

It felt good to drive again. The grey road unfolded beneath Kel's wheels, carrying her away from the hateful, silent street.

The sat nav soon urged Kel to get back on the main road and Kel took pleasure in calling it useless before yanking the power cable.

15 years ago

We wanted to be like teenagers in all the American films we watched. A campfire in the woods, marshmallows roasting, kissing games. We managed a disposable barbecue lit with a cigarette lighter and marshmallow goop all over pine cones. Close enough.

There were three girls and three boys which should have been perfect, but Rosie was sulking and wouldn't look at Mark, who was tossing marshmallows into Asad's waiting mouth. I leaned back into my current boyfriend, Greg, for a kiss. Not just to wind Rosie up, but to show the others he was mine. Especially Lola, who Greg kissed first while we were all drunk on WKD vodka in her swimming pool.

Rosie had always been funny about me kissing boys. The others said she was frigid and thought you got pregnant from kissing, even though she'd put condoms on bananas with the rest of us. But instead of revelling in the joy of such an easy lesson, she'd been sullen and sour-faced. Sometimes I thought she was more of a habit than a friend.

'This is nice, innit?' said Greg. He fed me some cremated marshmallow and I swallowed quickly to get the burnt taste out of my mouth.

'Let's tell ghost stories,' said Lola.

'It's not dark yet.'

The evening sun was full and strong, even through the trees. Three more weeks until school started again. It felt like we had forever.

'I'm not allowed out after dark,' said Rosie. 'It's not fair if I miss the stories.'

The group looked to me and I nodded. Rosie would cheer up if we told stories. Maybe then she'd be in the mood to entertain Mark and everything would be perfect, the way it was meant to be. The three prettiest, most popular girls in the year with the three sportiest, handsomest boys.

'Why don't you go first, Rosie.'

She nodded, took a deep breath.

'Listen,' Rosie intoned, darkly quiet, 'and you might just hear it.'

All we could hear was the crackle of flames, the rustle of leaves, the chirp of birds. Not particularly threatening noises. We exchanged puzzled glances.

'There!' she said. 'Did you hear?'

'No,' I said, already thinking about my story instead.

'Hoofbeats.'

'How is a fucking horse scary?' demanded Asad. 'Is it mad it didn't get enough hay or have its mane braided or something?'

I laughed, because a horse seeking revenge did seem pretty funny. I knew they had a wicked bite, but when you could choose a story about absolutely anything, a demented horse is disappointing.

'Not a horse,' said Rosie. 'A half-man, half-horse creature. With no skin! So you can see the muscles and organs and bones pulsing away inside. The trees cannot save you, as the beast fells them with its mighty axe. There is nowhere for you to run. Any moment, we may all be trampled by its great hooves.'

'What if we feed it marshmallows,' suggested Greg. 'Horses have a sweet tooth.'

'It yearns only for human flesh,' Rosie said testily.

'Which part eats you, the horse or the man?' I asked.

'Both!'

'Nah, I don't buy it. The digestive system would be completely stupid.'

I could see Rosie getting frustrated, but whatever. It's not my problem her story was rubbish.

April 2020, 1 month after COVID-19 lockdown

Kel usually wouldn't drive deep into London like this, but the roads were deserted. She flew by quiet streets, closed shops, darkened lights. She had to stop a few times to let urban foxes cross in front of her. They blinked their big brown eyes at her car and twitched their ears before bolting at the sound of her horn.

In the footwell of the passenger seat, buried under her coat, lay a shotgun. It was unlicensed, obtained via an online forum where money spoke louder than principles. The foxes were testing her patience, but she needed to save her shots.

Driving down the tree-lined Mall which Kel had only seen on TV, felt surreal. The streets were empty. The parks were empty. But she had no time to marvel. A flash of blue lights in her rear view mirror made her stomach drop. The police. She pulled over, with a nervous glance at her coat. They wouldn't search her car would they?

The car pulled in behind her. An officer got out. He had a walkie-talkie sticking out of his vest. She wound down her window.

'Where are you off to, young lady? No one's meant to be out and about. Now's not the time to be selfish. Think of those poor doctors and nurses.'

It was hard for Kel to summon pity for her doctor, a lumpy woman who held in a sigh whenever Kel dared go for an appointment.

'I'm going to my grandmother's down Rydon Lane,' she improvised, trying to sound innocent. 'She's all alone.'

'You've gone past it, love. Way past it. Can't blame you for sneaking a look at how empty it is smack bang in the middle of the city I suppose. Here, you can follow me if you like.'

Kel grit her teeth. 'Um. I wouldn't want to bother you.'

'No bother. I'll go ahead, there should be enough room to turn around and follow.'

Kel nodded. She waited for the officer to move his vehicle

out. Her hands paused on the wheel. She could make a three-point turn and follow him. Pretend the emptiest looking house on Rydon Lane was her grandmother's and wave him off. But what if he waited until she went in?

Sod it. She put her foot down. The car revved and shot forwards, in the opposite direction. She moved through the gears, watching the speedometer climb from forty to fifty to sixty. The police car would be too slow to turn and give chase. The siren rang out. She needed to get out of sight but the road seemed to go on forever.

She hit Trafalgar Square, ran all the red lights the way she'd always yearned to, slammed past Charing Cross. She saw an entrance to an underground car park, a gap in the buildings on her right. She leaned hard on the wheel and screeched inside, bumping against the narrow wall.

Kel parked and inspected the damage. The front bumper had taken a few knocks. The tyres seemed surprisingly intact. The sound of the siren whizzed past outside. He hadn't seen her. She was safe for now.

She grabbed her gun from the passenger footwell.

Let the unicorn hunt begin.

15 years ago

Lola told a story about a succubus. Asad went for zombies. Greg came up with an insane football player who kicked people's heads off. Mark did a bakery where human innards were disguised as cakes.

My story was about a girl who got lost in the woods with her boyfriend. The boyfriend became a ghostly wraith who hunted her down and gave her a half-human, half-wraith pregnancy. I put a lot of work into the gory details of the wraith child eating up its mother's ovaries. Rosie started looking sick.

'Let's maybe leave it there,' suggested Greg, chucking me under the chin. 'Keep the rest inside your gorgeous, twisted mind.'

'What should we do then?' I pouted.

'Obvious, isn't it? Kiss chase,' said Lola. She batted her eyelashes at Greg.

'What, like we're ten years old?' asked Rosie.

'We can do it, like, ironically,' said Asad. Utter bullshit but it was clear he was up for it. And so were the others. Even Rosie gained a certain mad glint in her eye. Maybe she liked a challenge when it came to kissing boys.

I eyed Lola. I could outrun her. She was a little fat around the thighs and didn't try too hard in PE. Thought she could play me, did she? No chance. As long as Greg was the top prize in our year, he was mine.

We gathered around the smouldering barbeque, each of us equidistant until I bellowed GO.

A blur of dashing limbs veered off into the forest. I legged it after Greg, branches snapping beneath my feet. The trail was tougher than I thought and I'd forgotten I was wearing stupid strappy shoes. I swore as the buckle snapped. My mum was going to kill me, I'd whined up a storm for these.

I couldn't be that far behind. I pushed my way through bushes which tore at my skirt, nettles stinging my skin. My heart thumped, my adrenaline surged. Kiss chase had been a great idea. A little pain would make the prize so much sweeter.

I burst out of the undergrowth into a fresh clearing. A

fairy circle of toadstools speckled the ground. Then someone grabbed me from behind. Spun me around. I closed my eyes. *Greg*. I thought his name like a prayer.

But the lips pressed to mine were too soft and slippery with lip gloss. My chin was pulled down instead of tilted up. Slender, dainty fingers. The kiss was neat and precise and tender, no slobber, no invasive tongue. I wished Greg kissed me like that.

It wasn't Greg.

When I opened my eyes I saw Rosie, blushing and breathless.

April 2020, 1 month after COVID-19 lockdown

Kel waited until dark and picked her way through the streets to her hunting ground. The only eyes she felt belonged to the lion statues at Trafalgar Square. She paused to take in the floodlit National Gallery, barricaded at the door. Any other spring evening would see small gatherings on the steps, tourists taking pictures. Now there was only emptiness.

The gun felt heavy. She hoped she could shoot using her left hand. Her right was scarred with a horn shape, twirling from the base of her wrist to her middle finger. The mark of someone cursed by a unicorn. Ridiculously, she thought of shooting cans at the fairground and winning a giant plush teddy.

The giant screens advertising drinks and holidays and clothes lit everything neon at Piccadilly Circus, endlessly flickering even with no one but her to see. Below ground, trains rumbled in the black tunnels. Cupid stood atop his statue, leg outstretched, bow in hand.

Kel sat at the base of the statue, gun concealed under her large black coat and waited. Cars flashed past every now and again. The time ticked up to midnight and beyond. Kel huddled into her coat as the air chilled.

How long until her parents tried to call and she didn't answer? Would her friends notice if she stopped replying to their messages? Would someone at Google notice the notifications stacking up in her inbox and realise she was missing?

It didn't matter. She'd rather die trying to lift her curse than live with it a moment longer. One foolish teenage moment in a unicorn's forest had ruined her, cursed her to be forever alone and she could no longer ignore it. It made her angry enough to want to watch something bleed.

Surely unicorns would be much more at home in a forest than the heart of a city. But now everything was quiet, there were more birds, more foxes, more rodents on every corner. So it made sense unicorns might be out and about as well.

Just as Kel was slipping into a doze, she heard the patter of hooves. *Clop clop clop.* She jolted awake and in the bright light, she saw the unicorn's shadow.

The unicorn had a rider. Long teenage limbs, a plait that wasn't quite straight, chunky trainers. Even before the name came to mind, Kel knew. Felt who the rider was in her bones, despite the impossibility. Her hands shook around the shotgun.

Rosie.

15 years ago

I wiped my mouth. Fury coursed through me.

'What do you think you're doing?'

'Given your boyfriend spends every moment you're not

looking with his tongue down Lola's throat, I thought you could do better...'

'That's not true! You—you twatwaffle!'

Rosie's mouth twitched upwards. She was laughing at me. Everyone was laughing at me. I gave her an almighty shove. She bonked ungracefully to the ground and laughed even harder.

I wanted to be cruel. I couldn't stop myself. The humiliation I felt would look so much better on someone else. For a moment, I didn't care that she was my best friend since we were eleven. And I forgot the kiss felt good, that she'd been both careful as well as careless. All I felt was a thick cocktail of embarrassment, shame, anger.

'You only want to get with a girl because no boy wants you.'

That did it. She stopped laughing. Looked more like I'd slapped her round the face.

'I know I shouldn't have done things this way, but don't you think the two of us make sense? I've loved you for so long, Kel.'

My head pounded. I couldn't take this. No, it didn't make sense. What made sense was three boys with three girls. Some people are gay, get over it. Fine. But me? No.

I turned, started stumbling back the way I came. Maybe I could still find Greg. Maybe I could still make things right.

I heard bellowing and yelling. When I reached the barbeque, Greg and Mark were grappling with each other, punching and kicking like animals. Lola looked at me smugly. They were fighting over *her*. I could have cried.

I threw myself into the fray. My target was Greg.

'You cheating son of a magpie murderer!'

The boys appeared surprised I wanted to join the violence. As I hurtled into them, I tripped over the barbeque. It shouldn't have mattered. The fire was almost dead.

At first we only watched as the flames licked up in a great *whumph*, scorching away the grass.

'Metal!' said Greg, tossing Mark aside. 'Someone pass me a marshmallow.'

Lola, ever his loyal servant, fumbled for the plastic bag with the sweets and skewers. A bolt of panic ran up my spine while they all seemed nonchalant, casual about the uncontrolled blaze spreading across the grass. I looked around for something we could use to put the fire out. I seized the closest bottle of water and doused the grass.

'Kel, no!' yelled Lola.

The fire leapt into life, consuming Mark's carelessly tossed jacket in a second. The boys leapt to get out of its way. Lola slapped me and I blinked, stunned as my cheek blossomed with pain.

'That's not water, you stupid bitch!'

I should have guessed that considering how silly the mood had turned. Even though we were now in serious trouble, I still felt hurt no one had bothered to offer me a swig. I guess they thought I'd go blabbing to Rosie.

The ground was dry. The grass was dry. We were surrounded by trees. Flames whooshed and billowed. I fumbled for my phone to call for help. No signal, God's sake. The smoke thickened, stinging my eyes, snatching my breath.

'Out!' said Asad, the only sensible voice among the lot of us.

A scamper of feet. I picked myself up, but twisted my ankle in my broken shoes. A spurt of pain shot up my leg and

I whimpered. They hadn't waited. The air was hot. The fire licked everything. My slapped cheek stung.

'Rosie!' I shouted, desperate, but I'd left her behind in the trees.

The fire was in front, behind, to the side. I didn't know which way to limp.

Then I saw something. A flash of white coat, a long horn. I thought of Rosie's monster.

But as it got closer, I saw it wasn't a monster at all. Storybook white, gleaming coat reflecting the orange flame. The unicorn appeared unbothered. He gave me a rueful look, like he knew it was all my fault.

I reached for the unicorn. He let me. 'Get Rosie,' I spluttered, grasping onto his horn. My hand burned at the touch, the pain whiting my vision. I took one last gasp of smoke-laden air before swinging myself onto his back.

April 2020, 1 month after COVID-19 lockdown

Kel remembered the lingering smoke over the village, lasting for days. Giving her statement to the police from a hospital bed while they treated her burns.

She'd fucking told that stupid unicorn to go back for Rosie and she knew he'd understood her. He hadn't listened. Why? Of course, telling anyone about the unicorn made them think she was mad. They'd asked over and over if she'd been smoking something that wasn't tobacco. Endless questions from police, press, parents.

The boys blamed her. Lola blamed her. She didn't go back to school. The only person who would have been on her side, Rosie, couldn't help her anymore. Because Rosie hadn't escaped the flames.

Or so Kel had thought. Her feet moved by themselves as she rose from the statue and walked, slowly, to where the unicorn waited.

Kel let out a sharp cry as the creature stepped from shadow into the light. Rosie's skin and hair were blackened, like the marshmallows they'd toasted that day. Her face was expressionless. There was no sign of the girl Kel had known. The gleaming white unicorn snorted and pawed the ground, as if to say, "Here she is, like you asked". Even though it was years too late.

'I'm sorry,' said Kel. Her cheeks were damp. If she could wind back time, she'd kiss Rosie back. Walk back with her to the others, tell them to stop fighting, finish the marshmallows, end the night in a sleepy, sugary haze.

Kel fumbled for the gun. Her shot rang clear in the night. It bounced off the creature's hide harmlessly, pinged into a nearby lamppost. Kel swallowed, hands shaking, trying to stave off her panic. The creature whinnied and charged. Kel threw herself down. The pavement rumbled beneath her cheek as another train passed below. She rolled, reached for her weapon, went to line up another shot.

'Wait,' the creature said. Rosie's voice, but creaking, distorted. 'I know you.'

She dismounted, stalked towards Kel, the unicorn on her heels. The smoky smell made Kel cough. Before her stood her best friend. Ripped clothes, flesh hanging in strips. Grotesque.

Kel did this.

'I thought the stupid unicorn would help you!'

Rosie said nothing for a long time. The unicorn snuffled

at her shoulder and Kel realised the unicorn had tried. It had left the curse on Kel so she could find it again. It had brought her Rosie, even if it was years too late to be of any help. Immortal creatures like unicorns must struggle to understand the concept of time passing.

'Kiss me,' said Rosie, as if she'd found the logical answer to a maths problem. She'd always known the value of x, had taught Kel her prime numbers.

But. Kiss this horrifying apparition of her old friend?

'I don't understand.'

'I never had anyone kiss me. Please, that's all I want.'

Kel closed her eyes. Rosie should have been a graduate, a girlfriend. And much more. So how could Kel deny her this?

She opened her eyes. She reached for Rosie's hand and felt heat emanating from her palms, hot enough to burn. She covered her hands with her coat sleeves and remembered the kiss in the forest. How careful Rosie had been. She moved her face closer. Touched her cool lips to Rosie's scorching ones. It hurt, but she bore the pain.

A flash of light. And when Kel's vision cleared, she saw the old Rosie looking back at her. The unicorn was there too, gleaming handsomely. Kel reached up unthinkingly to pet his mane. The unicorn touched his horn to Kel's hand. This time it didn't burn her. Instead, the mark from fifteen years ago faded away.

Kel stood alone in Piccadilly Circus. Her body ached. Her eyes burned. The thousands of words she'd kept in for so long loosened on her tongue, ready to spill over.

A kiss had always been the storybook way to break a curse.

The Last Fey Artist

Grigor was the third person I'd kissed and the one I'd kissed the longest. To look at, he was nothing special, muddy features in a thin face. But to kiss, he was very lovely indeed. And when he smiled, even better.

A sofa cushion dug into my back. I tossed it aside. The cushions and the sofa were the first pieces of furniture we chose together. The sofa had been a tragic case sagging in a charity shop, but we soon had it scrubbed up, cosy blankets draped all across the back to hide the scuff marks. I was thinking about painting them, turning them into something beautiful. I loved beautiful things, of course, but what I loved even more was the act of transforming something ugly.

Grigor picked up my hand and pressed his lips to the inside of my wrist. My veins gave off a gentle glow. Grandad married a *gwragedd annwn*, a lake fairy, so I'm part-fey. Not that I go around telling everyone I'm a fairy. It's only cute when you're six years old.

'You're so sweet,' Grigor said.

I mock shoved him. 'I am *not* sweet. I am a girlboss who just opened her first art exhibition. My work is "ethereal and evocative", I'll have you know.'

'Your head isn't going to fit out the door tomorrow. You'll just have to stay in my bed forever.'

I breathed out a noise like "Oh no" and then he kissed me until I was gooey and gasping. We probably should have left the sofa when the timer for the pizza went off, but kissing Grigor seemed far more important than frizzled pepperoni.

***

Calling it an "exhibition" was being generous. It wasn't in a proper gallery. It was at the local community centre, attended mostly by old folk desperate for something to do on a Sunday morning. Or desperately in need of sausage rolls. One man took a thirty-second cursory look at the first canvas before loading his paper plate at the buffet table.

April, an angel with excellent taste in art, and the local community events manager, smiled and tried to get him to appreciate my giant watercolour landscape. It had taken weeks of carefully dabbing trees and flowers into bloom so the colours blended just right. Each one was perfectly placed, every dab of paint and shade of green carefully orchestrated...

Most people went 'Oh, a flower field, that's nice' and walked right by it. The ingratitude was completely ordinary but still hard to swallow. Part of the problem is that art is everywhere, all the time. If only the world were rendered in greys, my work would be wildly popular.

My excitement began to wane as people had a cursory look around before helping themselves to the food.

'It's early yet,' April said, squeezing my arm. 'I've got the local paper coming later, that will get people interested.'

I gave her a wan smile. Everyone's got to start somewhere, I know that.

As an artist you have two choices: starve, or make artistry your side hustle. I have opted for the side hustle, plus extra help from Grigor. He is something important in cybersecurity which means he is on an obscene salary. He talks a lot about some guy called Roger. If his job is going well, Roger is a superstar, an all-conquering hero. If it is going badly, it is all Roger's fault for inventing such stupid systems.

Grigor turned up at the exhibition looking very cute in his green raincoat. He peered around and went straight for the painting I'd worked on with him. I couldn't help smiling as I remembered our Sunday afternoon routine. We piled all my art stuff into his tiny Peugeot and drove into the hills. I'd set up my canvas and paint while he read one of his long fantasy novels with incredibly complicated royal families. We both liked doing quiet activities together, one of the things I loved best about him. There was never any pressure to fill the air with empty talk.

Overcome with affection, I went and put my arms around him. He pulled me in for a close hug.

'You're incredible,' he said. 'I'm so proud of you.'

Suddenly it didn't matter that I wasn't grandstanding at a posh London gallery with people in suits writing me massive cheques. This was all I needed.

***

I sold four pieces, which made enough to cover materials and have a meal out with Grigor.

We went for an Italian. It wasn't often that I got to treat him. He happily hoovered up a big lasagna and several slabs of garlic bread.

'Rent's going up again,' he said, faux casually.

I worked part-time because my artwork only brought in a pittance. I wanted to keep it that way so I had more time to paint, but I knew I should ask.

'We're still alright though, with your salary?'

'Yeah. Course. Just thought you should know.'

He looked twitchy. I didn't want to say it. But maybe if I did, it would be good enough and we could move on to more interesting topics. I wanted to visit an aquarium and see if they would let me study underwater plants. My last exhibition had been earth themed and I'd decided on water for my next one. I brimmed with ideas and hoped Grigor might want to come on research trips with me. Art was often a solitary undertaking and it would be nice to have company.

'I can see about doing more hours, if that would help.'

'Nah'. He took another big mouthful of garlic bread. 'You need to start work on your next exhibition, right?'

I mentally breathed a sigh of relief. 'That's right.'

I was about to say more, when he continued—'It's a lot of work, isn't it, for one meal out.'

'It's not about the money. We've talked about this.'

'I know, I know. I'm sure one day you'll be the one making our fortune. The next Van Gogh.'

He meant well, but I could tell by his tone he didn't truly believe it. He was patronising me. A thrum of anger heated my veins. It was unpleasant. We'd been having such a nice meal and I didn't want to ruin it.

'Hey,' said Grigor, eyes suddenly wide. 'Your hands!'

I looked down and saw silver sparks dancing over my wrists. I thrust my hands under the table. 'Trick of the light.'

I hoped he couldn't hear the crackling, or perhaps thought it was background noise.

'You don't have special powers do you? Like, can you throw lightning?'

'I'm not a superhero,' I snapped. 'It's nothing. A trick of the light, like I said. Let's get dessert.'

He shrugged. 'Sure. Let's get the gelato.'

***

I was soon distracted from my annoyance with Grigor by a phone call from my Auntie Carys. She was my grandmother's oldest friend and liked to keep in touch. My grandad always called her *that woman* and spoke disapprovingly of her three ex-husbands, her custom-built bungalow and her "hippy-dippy" clothes. I always had the feeling there was more to the animosity between them, but he would never outright confess to it. My mum said he was jealous of the close friendship Auntie Carys shared with his wife. She could remember them bent together laughing at Sunday lunches, both Grandad and Carys's current husband left on the edge of things.

'El, my darling, do you think I could pop round and see your paintings? I'm doing a coach trip up your way and I'm sure I could toddle off for a tick.'

I stifled a laugh. Sure, Auntie Carys was doing well for her age but I doubted she was up to clacking up the hill we lived on, even with her best walking stick. 'I'll pick you up, Auntie. Just let me know when and where.'

***

Auntie Carys looked odd in our flat, like a lost time traveller. She belonged somewhere with high ceilings, wood panelling, sweeping staircases and grand family portraits in golden frames. Our landlord-mandated white walls and IKEA furniture didn't seem grand enough for her.

She was polite, accepting a mug of PG Tips and munching through a plate of shortbread fingers. Grigor made enquiries about her coach trip, her bungalow and if she was thinking of getting married again. At that, she laughed. 'I've had enough disappointment for one lifetime. It's the turn of you young people now. When are you walking down the aisle?'

Grigor choked on his tea. 'Um. Well. We haven't really discussed it.'

Auntie Carys raised a perfectly plucked eyebrow. 'Don't hang around too long, our Elin's got plenty of options.'

'Auntie! Stop teasing! We're happy as we are at the moment, but if that changes you'll be the first to receive an invitation.'

She stirred another sugar lump into her tea. 'I will hold you to that, my darling. Now, where are your paintings?'

***

My "studio" was our spare bedroom. The floor was covered in old sheets to protect it. A stack of blank canvases leaned in one corner, ready to be transformed. A giant pinboard contained quick studies and pages ripped from magazines. My current work-in-progress stood in the centre of the room. I needed a small step ladder to reach the top of the canvas and the giant easel had taken us far too long to put together. I found large canvases were the best way to truly get lost in a piece of work. I loved to hide tiny details no one would ever find—a flower with one extra petal, a bright streak of purple in the grass, a vaguely cat-shaped cloud.

Auntie Carys recognised the painting immediately. 'It's our lake!' she exclaimed. 'How lovely!'

When I was very young, our family, which included Auntie Carys and her current husband, always headed to the lake every year. We travelled deep into the middle of nowhere—no telephone poles, no stone walls, no sheep, not even a real road. We bounced along a dirt track in Grandad's big jeep, tree branches brushing the windows. I always felt scared, closed off from the sun and sky. When the light reached us again, we'd be at the lake which always shone the deepest of jewel blues. We'd camp there for a week with no contact with the outside world. The night sky was the greatest wonder; a dark canvas scattered with trails of sequins winking silver in the dark. When the lake's clear waters reflected the sky, it looked as if the whole world were made of stars.

I had attempted to recreate this. It was...a work in progress.

'I've been wanting to go back, but I'm not sure a bog-standard Peugeot will make it down the dirt track. Maybe we could hire something.'

'Don't go getting yourself in trouble trying to find it. That young man of yours has got all the sense of a chocolate teapot.'

'Auntie! Grigor's top of his field, he's got a first class degree.'

'Got to be careful with those high intelligence, low wisdom sorts.'

'He's not that bad, Auntie. And even if he were, he does really love me. Supports my art, thinks I'm talented, spoils me rotten.'

'Well. As long as he makes you happy.'

Auntie picked up my hand and squeezed it tight. 'Your grandma would love this, you know. She was always quite the artist herself, had her own drawings of the lake. I'm sure I've still got some tucked away. I'll send them to you, if you like.'

'I would love that. Thank you.'

'My pleasure. Shall we have a look at some more?'

I hesitated. 'Auntie. It happened again. You know, the light and the...' I attempted a noise like paper being scrunched up.

'Dear oh dear. Were you angry?'

'I could feel all this...energy...with nowhere to go.'

'That's why you've got your painting, isn't it? So you can put it all in there.'

'It's not enough.'

Auntie Carys put her hands on my shoulders. 'If you're angry you need to walk away. Sometimes husbands and boy-friends do stupid things. And that can lead to stupid thoughts like, "I wish you would forget about the blinking dishwasher." Then, because of your blood being up, your magic comes out to play. You know the rest.'

I knew. My mother always thought the fate of Auntie Carys's first husband particularly hilarious, although she never laughed about it to her face.

'Do you think Harold's new wife gets sick of explaining the dishwasher to him every day?'

'I don't give a flying frog, she's welcome to him. I'd cursed him to pieces by the time he left. Your grandma always had complete control over her magic though, the same control you've got.'

'Right, of course. So I should be fine.'

'I certainly hope so. You don't want Grigor thinking a bomb is about to go off whenever a Queen song comes on or communicating exclusively in Donald Trump tweets. Be like your grandma, not like me.'

***

I went back to the studio after Auntie Carys left, contemplating the lake painting. I surrounded myself with palettes covered in blues that were too pale, too deep, too murky. I couldn't find a blue that was *enough* and I was wasting paint.

Grigor came in as I started mixing yet another batch. He had a cup of tea and a sheepish smile.

'Ah. Still stuck on this one then.'

'None of them are *right*.'

'That blue looks nice,' he said inanely, pointing to the nearest palette. I wanted to throttle him for being so glib and casual. Then I took a deep breath and thought of Auntie Carys's ex-husbands.

Grigor put a hand up to his neck and rubbed it, frowning. 'Felt something just shock me. All staticy-like. Weird.'

Oh no. I took a long sip of warm, calming tea. Focus. 'If I could only go back to the lake, I'm sure I could get this colour right.'

'We can go anywhere you want. Just say the word and we'll make it into a proper mission.'

Grigor's earnest expression made me soften. Alright, he didn't understand the finer points of artistry, but he still cared about me and wanted to make me happy.

***

We hired a massive car, packed it up with art supplies and

headed out into the pouring rain. Water slashed across the windscreen and turned everything into green-grey sludge, but Grigor didn't let it deter him. We cranked up our playlist and sang along, drowning out the patter and rush of the downpour. The buildings and signs and street lights soon fell behind us. I loved the feeling of leaving the ordinary world behind. Work, rent, cleaning and cooking felt like old and distant dramas.

We trawled through the rain and mud until we reached the dirt track. Some of the trees had been cut down, but I felt a strange pull, as if the lake were calling me. The rain reduced to drizzle and then spit as we grew close.

I watched Grigor's face as we emerged into a splash of sunlight and could finally see the great, sparkling expanse of lake water. He looked enraptured. When I kissed him, he turned those same eyes on me.

'It's more beautiful than I expected,' he said.

We got my art kit out and set it up to my liking so I could begin my studies. While I started to work on colour mixing, Grigor circled the lake with his phone, taking picture after picture. Not being able to hear cars or trains made everything feel peaceful and still.

Evening drew in and we cooked a simple meal on a campfire. Then the stars rose and set everything alight, just like I remembered. With no street lights, their shine was the brightest thing around. I wished I could see this every night.

'This will be the centrepiece of my next exhibition,' I explained. 'I'll put it on the biggest canvas. I have a few ideas for the smaller ones too. Something with fish, I think. And a ship on the sea, ready to be pulled under the waves. Water can heal and hurt. Not enough, you die—too much, you drown. I want to capture all of that volatility in my work.'

'Sounds marvellous,' said Grigor. 'What about painting a cute seal?'

I laughed. 'Well, they live in water I suppose...'

'Everyone likes seals, I bet you could make one adorable enough to start a bidding war.'

'I'll give it some thought.'

'Thank you for showing me this. Today's been perfect.'

'I always wanted to have my honeymoon here one day...'

'Yeah. That'd be sweet. It's such a romantic spot.'

I kissed him, long and lingering. Then I closed my eyes, leaned into him and dreamt of a shining future where I took the art world by storm. As I was accepting my prestigious awards, I would say, "The biggest thank you goes to my darling husband Grigor."

***

After our trip, I began to work on the lake canvas in earnest. It had been too big to transport in the car, so I used the studies I'd done on smaller canvases to get the colours and shapes right. The evening hours drained away as my progress inched forwards.

Grigor usually spent evenings watching TV or tapping at a video game controller, but downstairs was silent. He'd been clicking away on his computer. I wondered if he was researching for another novel he would end up abandoning. I fervently hoped it was for something more wedding-shaped.

When I next came in from work on one of his work-from-home days Grigor immediately enveloped me in a hug. 'Missed you. House is too quiet.'

'Missed you too,' I said, dropping my bag so I could hold on to him.

'I've got a surprise for you.'

I could see it in my mind's eye. A deep black velvet ring box.

'Should I get changed first?'

'As long as you wear this.'

He produced his sleeping mask. Cute. Maybe he'd made up the room. Hopefully nothing too over-the-top. I didn't want to be picking glitter out of my food for weeks.

'I can do that.'

'Call when you're ready.'

I chose the dress I felt most confident in, black with crimson floral accents and draped sleeves. I applied more makeup than my everyday look, used a brighter lipstick as no doubt we'd be snapping pictures for Auntie Carys.

Once I was done, Grigor carefully led me through the house. Before long, I could smell the homely, paint-y smell of my studio. Having both my loves in one room for the proposal struck me as shockingly romantic. I knew Grigor sometimes didn't *get* my art, which made it even more touching.

'Ready?'

I nodded. Grigor whipped off my blindfold.

'Ta-dah! I thought we could sell them as greetings cards or put them on the cover of notebooks, as it's all digital.'

I blinked. Grigor had moved things about in the studio, displaying a series of prints on the massive pin board. I saw a ship on crashing waves. Goldfish in a pond. The massive round eyes and whiskers of a seal. And worst of all, the lake, rendered in a silver and navy scatter of stars. My stomach plummeted. Why was my studio full of art that wasn't mine? Was this meant to be some sort of misguided attempt at inspiration?

'It's your next exhibition,' said Grigor, eyes alight and excited. 'This is the kind of thing you wanted to make, right? So I put everything you made so far into an AI programme and bam—all the art came out in no time at all!'

I moved closer to the image of the lake. The composition matched my unfinished canvas, but this was a completed piece. Hours of work reduced to seconds. The computer knew how much I wet my brushes, the angle I lay my strokes, how to mix my favourite colour palettes. It had absorbed a piece of my soul and there was no way for me to reclaim it. I couldn't begin to explain the depth of Grigor's betrayal, the violation of everything I thought we had together.

'How dare you, Grigor Morgan.' My tone was low, dangerous.

His smile slipped. 'I don't understand.'

Tears flooded my cheeks. I had been looking forward to working on new art for this exhibition and Grigor had gone and done it all for me. My ideas felt ruined now that I'd seen the computer productions.

It wasn't only mimicking. It was crueller than that. The images had been made so people would *like* them. Especially that stupid seal. I'd always wonder if they were better than my own. Maybe they were. Maybe no matter my skill, the computer would always win more approval. It could work faster than me, pull down data about millions of paintings in seconds and use it to create new pieces in my exact style.

'I only wanted to help you, El, please don't cry—'

I could hear crackling. I could see Grigor's eyes fixed on my hands, where I knew light gathered in bursts and bolts. I knew I needed to shut up, stop talking, walk away. But I couldn't. A hurricane of anger overtook me.

'You have no idea what real beauty is,' I screamed out.

A flash and a pop like thunder. My skin buzzed and my vision sharpened. I could taste the magic in the air, feel it crawling all around me.

Grigor blinked rapidly. 'What...? You look strange all of a sudden. Sort of dull. Ordinary.'

I should have cared. But hurt and betrayal stung me hard with every breath. Love was buried too far underneath my storming emotions. Nothing mattered to me anymore. I could never be with someone who'd so profoundly misunderstood me.

'I don't look beautiful anymore, do I?'

Grigor shook his head, as if trying to shake off a bad dream. He would never again enjoy the azure sky on a summer's day or wild flowers rainbowing across the fields in spring. He'd never appreciate the rich green of the hills or the red glow of a perfect sunset. He'd never again be honestly able to tell me I was beautiful. Or anyone else for that matter. He could no longer see beauty. He was my first love and my first curse.

***

I gathered up my brushes and palettes and pots. Packed up my canvases. I no longer saw the point of my craft, not when a computer could mock up a thousand perfect paintings in a second. And not just any paintings, *my* paintings.

Once I was an artist. Not anymore.

'You're coming back,' said Grigor, watching me snatch up his car keys. 'This is just a misunderstanding.'

I drove in an uncaring haze. I wasn't sure where I was going until I stared out at the still surface of the lake, the pool of stars exactly how I remembered. The car was battered and mud-stricken but I'd made it.

I unloaded the car and began to throw my paintings into the lake. I watched each one sink beneath the shining water, lost forever.

ORIGINS OF THE MYTHS

The Myths

The Gremlins of RAF Wick*

The Loch Ness Monster

The Cauld Lad of Hylton Castle

The Fairy Tree of County Clare

The Swaffham Pedlar

The Elfin Cow of Llyn Barfog

The Lantern Men of Wicken

The Gremlins of RAF Benson*

The Knucker of Lyminster

The Gremlins of RAF St Eval*

The Mermaid of Zennor

*Online sources jointly credit Royal Air Force bases St Eval, Benson and Wick for legends about Gremlins

Jack Frost and The Green Man can be found in legends throught the UK.

Unicorns are the national animal of Scotland and can be found in heraldy and other historical artifacts across Scotland

Jack Frost and the Green Man

Jack Frost is said to be an icy spirit with a mischievous streak. He likes to ice up the inside of people's windows during winter, as well as leave frostbite on fingers and toes.

The Green Man brings life to flowers and plants during spring. His image is seen carved into many old buildings around the UK—a man's face surrounded by leaves. His image was included on invitations to King Charles III's coronation in 2023.

The Knucker of Lyminster

A knucker is a dragon or a serpent-like creature living in a deep pool of water called a knuckerhole. These pools can be found all over the English landscape.

The Knucker of Lyminster demanded the village sate its appetite with livestock and pretty maidens, and so an ordinary village lad decided to try his hand at monster slaying. He did not do this with a sword, as in tradition. Too many had tried that and been eaten. He opted for the more cunning method—offer the beast a poisoned pie.

The knucker ate the pie and died. The lad became a hero. However, he went down the pub for a knees-up to celebrate without washing the poison from his hands. He ingested it and ended up just as dead as the knucker.

In Lyminster, you can see The Slayer's Slab in St Mary Magdalene's Church. This is supposedly the tomb of the knucker slayer.

The Loch Ness Monster

In 2019, scientists from New Zealand analysed the DNA of creatures living in Loch Ness. Their analysis concluded that the most plentiful residents of the lake were eels, with no sign of any reptile or amphibian DNA that could explain the presence or origins of Nessie.

Many have attempted to photograph Nessie over the years. The most famous photograph, the "surgeon's photograph" from 1934, was confirmed as a hoax. A toy submarine from Woolworths and some wood putty stood in for the monster. The photograph was sold to the *Daily Mail* as an elaborate act of revenge by a disgraced journalist.

Tourists and experts are still searching for Nessie.

The Pedlar of Swaffham

The pedlar had a strange dream. A man told him that if he went to London Bridge, he'd find his fortune. So the pedlar duly packed up and travelled to London by horseback, his faithful dog by his side. On London Bridge, he met another man. The man told the pedlar he had a dream about a house in a strange place called Swaffham. He dug up the garden and found a box of gold! So the pedlar went home, dug up his garden. And sure enough he found gold.

The Hungry Ghosts

The Hungry Ghost festival is celebrated by Chinese communities. People leave out food for the spirits of their family to stop them from becoming hungry ghosts, which is a worse fate than hell. During the month of the festival, children are warned not to stay out after dark. People also avoid swimming or driving at night.

The Lantern Men of Wicken Fen and Black Shuck

The Lantern Men of Wicken Fen enticed lost and weary travellers off the pathways by shining their lantern lights. They lured the travellers into the bogs and drowned them.

People were warned not to whistle, believing this may attract the attention of the Lantern Men.

Travellers were advised to throw themselves face down in the mud, whistle back and forth with a fellow traveller or leave behind a light source in order to evade their clutches.

Included in the same story, Black Shuck was a dog-like beast said to roam East Anglia as an omen of death.

The Cauld Lad of Hylton Castle

The Cauld Lad is said to be the ghost of Robert Skelton, a stable boy. It was rumoured he was murdered by Baron Hylton, but the baron was never convicted. He claimed the boy had fallen and died from his injuries.

Shortly after this, strange happenings began in the castle kitchen. It would be messed up during the night, with chamber pots emptied all over the floor. The cook stayed up to catch the troublemaker and saw the ghost, who cried that he was cold.

The cook left a coat out for the boy and the ghost stopped causing trouble for the cook.

The Gremlins

A World War II RAF pilot stared at the mechanisms inside his plane. The vehicle was malfunctioning, but why? Must be those pesky gremlins he'd been warned about.

The gremlins starred in some cool 1940s era health and safety posters advising that if you forgot to do things such as wear safety goggles, the gremlins would take the opportunity to throw oil into your eyes. Many pilots lived in fear of the malicious creatures meddling with their equipment and causing fatal accidents.

The Fairy Tree of County Clare

In 1999, engineers desperately worked on a project to build a new bypass on the M18 motorway in County Clare, Ireland. The project met widespread protest by locals, as it would destroy a hawthorn fairy tree.

Local legend had it the tree was a fairy war ground and if humans interfered, the warring fairies would join forces against them. Storyteller and folklorist Eddie Lenihan warned that harming the tree would lead not only to bad luck, but to people being killed on the motorway.

The long-suffering engineers worked around the tree while building the new road and to this day the tree still stands. The uproar around the tree caused the project to be delayed by ten years. The story gained international attention.

There are many ash and hawthorn fairy trees dotting Ireland. It is believed that disturbing the trees can lead to a lifetime of bad luck.

The Mermaid of Zennor

The mermaid came to the church in Zennor every week to hear the voice of one of the local choir boys. She always sat in the same chair, which still stands in the church. One day, the boy went with her.

They were never seen again.

Then, a sailor came back with a tall tale. A mermaid asked him to move the anchor of his ship, as it was blocking her doorway and she needed to get back to her children.

The mermaid had married the choir boy and started a family with him under the water.

Unicorns

A white horse with a mythical horn which is said to have great healing powers. They are attracted to virgins and are a symbol of purity. Killing unicorns, even by accident, has grave consequences.

It is the national animal of Scotland, believed to be a worthy rival for the English lion.

The unicorn has become a symbol of magic and rarity. It has also been adopted by queer communities as the experience of being a minority can be lonely and isolating.

The Elven Cows of Llyn Barfog

The beautiful lake Llyn Barfog in Snowdonia, Wales is surrounded by many legends. It was even said to have been visited by King Arthur, who slayed a monster there.

The lake is said to be home to *gwragedd annwn*, beautiful fairies who live underneath the water. Legend has it the fairies looked after elven cattle. One escaped and was found by a local farmer, who quickly found the cow's milk yielded the tastiest cheese, butter and milk for miles around.

The farmer became rich by selling the milk as well as the cow's offspring. When the farmer sent the now elderly original elven cow to the butcher, the butcher's knife passed straight through its head. A woman in green, one of the *gwragedd annwn,* then called the cow and all its offspring back under the lake.

Only one cow remained behind. It had a black coat. This was the first Welsh black cow.

Acknowledgements

Special thanks to Maisie, Simone, Leigh, Annika and Shirley who provided invaluable help beta-reading, editing, proofreading and formatting the stories. I would never have finished this collection without your continued support and encouragement.

Thanks also to Kate Worsley for mentoring me on the Escalator Development Programme and making me believe my ideas were worth writing about. And also thanks to the fabulous team at the National Centre for Writing. You have changed my life. I was about to give up on writing. Then your acceptance came into my mailbox.

Finally, thanks to my parents for being kind and supportive of the project.

About the Author

Melody writes short stories based on myths and legends from the UK and beyond and is particularly interested in mythical creatures. She lives in Cambridgeshire where she works as an IT technician.

She was mentored by Kate Worsley on the National Centre for Writing's Escalator Development Programme in 2022 which culminated in reading her work to industry professionals at Dragon Hall, Norwich. Her work has been featured in publications from Noctivagant Press, Comma Press and Knight Writing Press.

Her website is at https://melodybowles.carrd.co/

Milton Keynes UK
Ingram Content Group UK Ltd.
UKHW050736051123
431993UK00006B/18